THIS WILL
BE
DIFFICULT
TO
EXPLAIN

and other stories

ALSO BY JOHANNA SKIBSRUD

Fiction
The Sentimentalists

Poetry
Late Nights with Wild Cowboys
I Do Not Think That I Could Love a Human Being

THIS WILL BE DIFFICULT TO EXPLAIN

and other stories

JOHANNA SKIBSRUD

W. W. Norton & Company
New York • London

For information about permission to reproduce selections from this book,
write to Permissions, W. W. Norton & Company, Inc.,
500 Fifth Avenue, New York, NY 10110

For information about special discounts for bulk purchases, please contact
W. W. Norton Special Sales at specialsales@wwnorton.com or 800-233-4830

Manufacturing by Courier Westford
Production manager: Anna Oler

Library of Congress Cataloging-in-Publication Data

Skibsrud, Johanna, 1980–
This will be difficult to explain : and other stories / Johanna Skibsrud. —
1st American ed. 2012
p. cm.
ISBN 978-0-393-07375-1 (hardcover)
1. Short stories. I. Title.
PR9199.4.S567T45 2012
813'.6—dc23

2011052860

W. W. Norton & Company, Inc.
500 Fifth Avenue, New York, N.Y. 10110
www.wwnorton.com

W. W. Norton & Company Ltd.
Castle House, 75/76 Wells Street, London W1T 3QT

1 2 3 4 5 6 7 8 9 0

CONTENTS

The Electric Man   1

The Limit   27

French Lessons   53

This will be difficult to explain   63

Clarence   83

Signac's Boats   97

Cleats   109

Angus's Bull   133

Fat Man and Little Boy   151

Acknowledgments   170

THE ELECTRIC MAN

For Rebecca

THE FIRST TIME I saw him he was sitting out on the deck of the Auberge DesJardins, drinking something out of a tall glass. He had a broad-brimmed straw hat on, the kind that women wear, and he was reading *The Herald Tribune*. I was always looking out for *The Herald Tribune* that summer, because it indicated to me the English-speaking visitors when they came. Though I could no longer excuse the great loneliness of that summer by the dearth of English newspapers in the place, I was always happy to see *The Herald Tribune*.

The Auberge was a spot more popular among the Continentals. The Americans and the Brits and even most of the Australians stayed at the bigger resorts, closer to town. We kept mostly Swiss and Belgian visitors, many of whom had been coming to stay at the Auberge for many years, and so were not—as the Americans always seemed to be doing—simply passing through.

By that point in the summer, my French was good enough for just about every purpose except being able to actually *say* anything. My accent was all right, the guests all said so: I could carry it off. It wasn't marvellous, they didn't say that, but they did say, to my credit, that I didn't sound like an American, pretending, or—and this was worse—a Canadian, being sincere.

When I saw him the first time I was doing the afternoon rounds on the deck—sweeping through, as I did every four o'clock—collecting empty glasses and trays and asking if the guests were quite as comfortable as could be expected. Everyone mostly said that they were. The Auberge—especially out on the deck, in the pre-dinner hours—was a comfortable place, and very few people thought to complain. Except, of course, on the occasion that they should need a drink, or the bill, or else another drink, and then they did ask, but so politely—in so light and detached a way—that it was as if they wished to indicate that the lack, indicated by the request, was in fact just another element from which was composed an all-around satisfactory whole. One or two guests, however, over the course of the weeks that I stayed on at the Auberge, could be counted on to be more exacting than most. The man with the hat was, it turned out, one of those.

THE FIRST TIME I saw him was not the first time he saw me, and when I made my way over to his table and said, "Tout va bien, Monsieur?" because he looked like a man who didn't need a thing in the world, he said, "Non." He said: "I saw you pass this way fifteen minutes ago, and I tried to get your attention. There's not enough ice in my drink." He rattled his tall glass so that I could see that it was true.

From his accent I guessed he was from somewhere in the Northeast. Connecticut, New Hampshire, maybe, and I thought it was too bad that he could tell right away that I wasn't French. Usually it was just the people who really *were* French who could tell. But maybe, I thought, he was one of those guests whose French was so bad they didn't even try. Who just spoke English as though they expected everyone to understand, or else learn in a hurry.

"I'm sorry, sir," I said, in my friendliest voice. "We'll get that fixed up for you right away," and he said, "I didn't expect you to be from the South. I would have pegged you as being from Minnesota or something. St. Paul. Aren't you a little serious," he said, "for the South?"

I didn't know what he meant, but I knew he didn't mean to be nice. He had a teasing, half-mean look in his eye and held his glass away from me when I leaned over to take it away. I could tell he was going to be a most scrupulous guest, and any hope that I'd had for striking up more than the usual conversation with him was gone. I just wanted to get back to the kitchen, to get him more ice for his drink like he'd asked.

The glass itself, however, the man with the hat had by then retracted—just enough that I would have had to really reach for it in order to take it away. He watched me carefully as he held it there, at that particular distance, looking interested in what I might do. I didn't do anything. I just stood there with my hand—not extended, but just open and waiting between us—until he got bored with the game and simply handed me the glass.

That's the way things went for some time. He didn't like me very much, and I didn't like him. Or else he liked me too much, and I didn't like him. I couldn't decide, and neither one pleased me.

I could never please him, either. I wasn't, perhaps, quite *authentic* enough for him. Whenever I answered his questions—about where I had come from and why—he always gave me a suspicious sideways look, as if he supposed I was lying and he and I both knew it but we weren't going to say anything about it—at least for a while.

He was the one who asked questions—I never volunteered information on my own. And he never believed what I told him. It gave me an uncomfortable feeling, because his questions were never particularly complicated, and I had never before had anyone doubt the answers I gave to questions as simple as those.

I SAW A LOT of the man with the hat after that. He stayed on at the Auberge for the final part of July and most of August. Unlike the other guests, he didn't go into town, or take weekend excursions to Provence or down along the Côte d'Azur. Like me, he stayed at the Auberge pretty much all of the time.

I would see him in the mornings in the dining room when I delivered curled-up butter to the tables, and then later I would see him down at the beach, sitting in one of the Auberge's folding chairs, his woman's hat on, when I went down to the shore to collect the beach furniture that had been abandoned by the other guests. In the late afternoons, I would always see him on the deck, before the dining room reopened—he was always very prompt at mealtimes—and I would laboriously refill his tall glass with ice that, it seemed, melted unnaturally fast in his hands.

One afternoon, I said to Marie-Thérèse, who was a niece of Madame and Monsieur Rondelle, the owners of the Auberge, and had worked in the dining room three summers in a row, "Il n'est jamais contente!" As I spoke, I tossed my hands in the air in order to emphasize my disdain for a man who could never be *contente* with a thing. I was always talking with my hands in those days—to make up, I suppose, for how I always suspected my words to fall so short of whatever it was I was trying to say. Marie-Thérèse just shrugged. She was a very easygoing girl, quite *contente* herself, almost all of the time. "Quelque personnes," she told me, "sont comme ça." She shrugged again, and went out onto the deck to check on a guest, who was just then at the very beginning stages of needing something.

The way she said it, "sont comme ça," as if it were the most inevitable and insignificant thing that it should be so, made me feel a little foolish for having allowed myself to be so bothered by the hatted man, who was—as Marie-Thérèse said a little later—obviously "un peu cuckoo." As she said it, she wound her finger as if around an invisible spool beside her ear, rolling her eyes up into her head so just the bottom bits of her irises showed.

IN THE EARLY AFTERNOONS, before I had to go up to the deck to refill the guests' drinks with ice, and take away and refill the trays with little things to eat, I would always go down to the beach myself, and lie out on one of the long fold-out chairs, in the shade. I always covered myself up completely, even in the shade, on account of my fair skin, which was so easily burned. I wasn't like the French girls who just got browner and browner as the summer wore on and could lie out from ten to two o'clock and not get burned, even on their most sensitive spots, which were also bare.

Because everyone else preferred the sun, I had my shady spots all to myself, and the beach felt secluded and private in the places that I chose. I liked it that way. It was a change from the constant hum of the Auberge, which was busy in the high season. Also, it made me feel as though, at least in those moments, I had control over my solitude. That it was a thing I had chosen.

Sometimes I would try to read, but I was allowing myself to read only French books during the day, and that was difficult. I could never get into the plot of anything. I understood the words, that wasn't the problem—it was just that that was all they seemed to be to me on the page. Just little, individual words—each one isolate, and independent of any of the other little words, which I also understood, and therefore not seeming to be continuous, in any broader sense, beyond their exact and independent meaning.

So after a little reading I would give up, and put the book down on the sand, and stare around at the beach and out to the water, which always looked very blue and warm, even though if I ever went down to it, it turned out to be cold. Also, it was green and brown up close, and not brilliant and blue as it had looked from afar.

For some time I was always re-convinced from a distance that the next time I went down to the water it would really be how it appeared. But after a while I stopped going down at all. I didn't like to keep finding that I'd—again—been wrong.

So I stayed up in the shady spot that I had all to myself instead, not reading, and just looking around. I had rediscovered an old habit of mine, which was to look at things through a narrowed field of vision by cupping my hand around my eye. In this way I would reduce the world to such a small point—my palm curled like a telescope, and one eye closed—that all I could see was one particular thing. For example, I would look out at the ocean and narrow my palm in that way so that all I could see, beyond my own hand, was a completely uniform shade of blue, uninterrupted by any other shade, or by any of the noise and commotion of the bathers, who stayed in the shallow parts, near shore. Or else I would turn my head and with my telescope eye see just the top bit of a sail. Or a radar reflector—glinting in the sun. Seeing neither, that is, the radar or the sun, but instead just—that *glinting*; just the reflection of metal and light.

It was, indeed, an old habit—back from when I was a kid, and would go out into the small front yard of my mother's house in Jacksonville and look at things like that, just a little at a time. After a while I knew the whole front yard that way—in small sections, each the size of a dime. What I liked best was to look at the natural things: the grass and the little scrubby flowering bushes in my mother's garden by the porch—and the sky. I could pretend that the rest of everything didn't exist. That I was a different sort of girl, who lived in the country instead of in town, and was surrounded by wilderness on all sides.

When I had chosen one unblemished spot, one particular, dime-sized part of the yard, I would concentrate on it very hard. I would try to press myself, every bit of myself, into that small space left between my palm and the curled-up pinky finger of my right hand. To rush right out of myself, just as—I imagined—that other girl, who was not me, and yet was ever so much more me than I myself could ever have been—might do.

It was a tingling, rushing, electric sensation that I felt coursing through my body then, when I tried so hard to push myself into the fragments of the lawn, and experience the world in the whole and real way that another (I imagined) might. Like maybe the little bits of me were on fire and if I didn't get pressed into the spot that I wanted to press myself into, I might burn up and be gone.

It seemed important. To be able to get into blades of grass the way that I wanted to. Or into the two or three spots in the sky that weren't marked up by tall houses, or telephone poles.

ONE AFTERNOON, down by the shore in front of the Auberge, just as I had set down my book that I wasn't really reading, the man with the hat came over and set up his chair next to mine. I saw him from a distance before he came. Before, that is, it was clear to me that it was in my direction, specifically, that he would come.

He was carrying his chair, and walked slowly, the chair banging on his leg with every second step. I made a tunnel of my right hand and held it up to my right eye, squinting the left so that it was entirely closed. Then I followed his hat, just the broad brim of his hat, until, when I took my hand away from my eye, I realized that he was almost upon me, and he could see very well what I was doing. I wiped my eyes, surprised, and then continued to do so as he approached, as if I hoped us both to believe that it was what I'd been doing all along. He put up his hand in greeting but didn't say anything until he had settled—quite near me—into his chair.

"Hello," he said, naturally. As if, outside of my working hours, he respected that I was in no way responsible for any discomfort of his.

"Hello," I said. But I was wary. I wondered what he would ask me, because he didn't have a drink, and I didn't have any ice.

"You probably don't know this about me," he said. "I'm a painter."

"Oh?" I asked, but he didn't say anything more. "That's interesting," I said. "What sort of painting do you do?"

"Landscapes mostly," he told me. Then paused again. "But I've been meaning"—he kept his eye on me as he spoke—"to try a portrait someday." Again he paused. "I was wondering," he said finally, "if you would be willing to sit for me someday soon."

Because I didn't have a proper reason to refuse, I said that I would, and the next evening, as we'd arranged, I knocked on the door of his third floor room. I could hear him shout from the inside that I should come in, so I did, and there he was, sitting in one of the straight-backed chairs that were provided in the more modest rooms. Next to him was a dish of watercolours and a small stretched canvas. He had been waiting for me. He didn't have an easel or anything, and his watercolours appeared unused. There was another straight-backed chair opposite him with an uneven table behind it. On the table was a small lamp that cast a limited light around the otherwise dim room. I had made—I thought suddenly—a rather large mistake. He wasn't a real painter, that was obvious now—and was perhaps even more *cuckoo*, as Marie-Thérèse had said, than we had originally supposed.

I thought it best if I left immediately. Quickly and discreetly. And in the future—I thought—be even more certain not to disturb, or trouble, the man with the hat. But instead of leaving, and for somewhat of the same reason that I agreed in the first place—because I could not think how to refuse—I sat down in the chair he had arranged for me, opposite his own.

"Let me guess," he said, after a while—he was sketching away at the canvas, with an ordinary pencil, his paints laid aside. Every now and then he would look up at me, but more often he looked down at the pencil. "Let me guess," he said. "You wanted to be an—actress when you were a girl."

It was not what I expected to hear. "No," I said. I never had wanted to be an actress. I supposed he'd said it imagining that all girls who agreed to sit for portraits imagined themselves that way, then or at some other, earlier time of their lives. That they were all aware, and wanted to be made more so, of their own particularness, their singularity.

I liked the movies, but the theatre seemed exaggerated to me. It always rang a little false. One time I'd gone up north to a festival in Savannah with my friend Ariane. We sat right up front for a production of *A Single Afternoon*, which was put on by a British company that Ariane had told me I'd enjoy. They were "naturalists"—like in the movies. "They even have the backstage set up to look like another room of the set," she explained. "So the actors don't get out of character between scenes."

I had never been more bored in my life. Even Ariane was bored. You could feel it—boredom everywhere. Soon even the actors started to feel it. They sped up their lines, and started to look angry, when it didn't seem "right" or "real" that they should.

Not even midway through, Ariane leaned over and said, "I'm depressed."

We were sitting so close to the stage that at a certain point—surely things were now drawing to a close—one of the actors came forward, so close that I could have reached up and touched him—and I did. Without really thinking— I did. I reached out and touched his foot, which was clothed in a very ordinary sock—the thick, pilly wool kind that lots of men wear, and that on occasion I had even worn myself.

Ariane, even with how into "making a scene" she was in those days, was horrified, and leaned away from me, as if in reflex. She looked at me from that new distance as though she had never seen me before in her life. It was no ordinary boundary, the look suggested, that I had crossed. The actor himself gave a kind of a jump when I touched him, and then shot me a startled and irritated glare. We were so close that I could see every line, and every slight change in the expression, on his face. He was older than he was pretending to be.

It was just: there was something ridiculous and sad about those socks. I wanted to touch them. All of a sudden, seeing them so close, all the little pilly hairs shooting off from them in all directions, I'd thought, isn't it the saddest thing in the world that there was this sock—what seemed to me the single realest sock I'd ever seen—up there, in front of me on the stage, and it was pretending *not* to be a sock, or at least to be a sock in *another* afternoon, a sock that it, so evidently, was not.

A sock that would be realer than the sock that it *actually was*, was a thing that I could not imagine.

I TOLD THE MAN with the hat that I hadn't ever wanted to be an actor. The closest I had come, I said, when he seemed surprised, was in a fourth-grade play when I was supposed to play a crow. "I didn't have any lines," I told the man. "I was just supposed to fly around in the background, but that was fine by me."

"I imagine you were a very good crow," the man said with a little smile. He had picked up his tray of paints and was beginning to dab at the canvas.

"I wasn't," I said. "I called in sick. My mother dressed me in the costume and painted my face, but then I looked in the mirror and started to cry. Nothing my mother could do could get me to leave the house looking like that."

"I guess I was wrong," the man said.

"I just kept saying," I told him, "'I don't want to be a crow! You can't make me!'" I laughed, but the man—who was not wearing his hat on this occasion—did not.

"That's sad," he said. His old sideways look was back. It

seemed his remark may have even been a sort of reproach. For laughing at something that he saw—and that I should see too—wasn't very funny at all.

Well, it was *my* story.

"Oh, it's okay," I said. I didn't think it was sad. "I thought I was supposed to be too *serious* anyway."

I WENT BACK TWO OR three more times to sit for the guest. In the daytime, we resumed our old routines, and he never mentioned anything about the painting when he saw me. Strangely, he didn't try to talk to me, either, as he had done before when I refilled his drink with ice in the late afternoons. He seemed more distant, and formal, as if we had never met at all, and that made me feel a little strange about the whole thing—as though I'd had a love affair with the old man, instead of simply sitting in a chair.

We acted like that with each other, for some reason. Overly polite and conventional like that. We didn't, either of us—as is often the case with the more humid matters of the heart—know quite how to understand the breach (though it had been, in our case, only the smallest, almost undetectable, tear) of our independence from one another, which we otherwise would have maintained.

ONE DAY, WHILE HE WAS working away without even looking up at my face, which often for long stretches he was able to do, I said, "Why did you think that? Why did you ask me that before—if I'd wanted to be an actress?"

He said only, as I had suspected: "Doesn't every young girl?" And shrugged. He did not seem in the mood to discuss anything.

But instead of letting the subject drop, as I might have, I said I didn't think all young girls *did* want to be actresses. I said it was an unfair thing to assume. I guess that I was feeling a little hurt, because I'd thought, if nothing else, that he was a man who paid attention to things. Who was perceptive, and had perhaps seen something in me, something particular, that had made him ask that question, instead of its springing from either mere supposition or form.

So maybe I liked, after all, the way that he looked at me sideways when I answered his questions, as if I thought for a moment, too, with that look, that I had made it all up— that the details of my life weren't really my own. That I was perhaps someone altogether different—whose particulars I didn't, or was just about to, know.

But later he said, "I myself was an actor, you know," and I said, "I thought you were a painter," and he said, "A person can be more than one thing."

"Okay," I said. "So what kind of actor were you?" He could be amusing after all.

"You just struck me," he said, in answer to my previous question, and ignoring the last, "like me in a way. Like someone"—he looked up for the first time in a while— "who wishes they were more than they are in real life, or at least something—somebody—else sometimes. That's an acting technique," he told me. "I suppose you wouldn't know that. Starting from zero so that then you can become something, or someone, entirely new." He was working away diligently with the paints, the small canvas tilted— always—up and away from me so that I couldn't see the progress that he made. "That's what you should have done when you were a crow," he told me. "Your problem was seeing yourself as a little girl who *looked* like a crow, and not being the crow yourself." I nodded, and made a small sound like I was interested, and understood. He didn't seem embarrassed at all to say what he had, and I did think *that* was interesting. What he said really did strike me as an essentially embarrassing thing to say. *To admit*, that is, that you were not, in and of yourself, *enough*. And would remain that way. To my American sense of things, which I—and I assumed that he, too—had retained (he had the accent, after all, stronger than my own), well, wasn't that the very worst thing that a person could admit?

"I don't think that's me," I told him quickly. "I think I'm all set to be just me. Just as I am."

"So I was wrong again," the man said, shrugging his shoulders again, like it was no big deal. "Just with me, it's different," he said after a while, "because I really was an actor."

"Right," I said. "What kind of actor did you say that you were?"

"A circus performer," the man said. "I was the Electric Man in the Bulgarian Circus."

I laughed even though he didn't. "The electric man?"
I said. I tried to become serious again, as if I had been all
along. "What's that?"

"Oh," he said, putting his paints aside. "Oh, you don't
know about that, either." And then he told me about how
it was to be an Electric Man in the Bulgarian Circus. How
every night he would go out into the ring, and put his hands
on a shiny metal ball, and be pumped through with electricity that the silver ball shot out so that his hair stood up on
his head and his clothes got singed and sometimes at the
end of the night he would have small wounds on the tips of
his fingers where the electricity had had nowhere else to go
in his body and so burned its way out. "The crowd loved me
the best," the man said. He never wore his hat in the room,
and he was bald as an apple. "I never saw it myself, from
my position, but they said that from the stands I *glowed*."

"That's just crazy," I said, but I was impressed. I didn't
know, of course, if I should believe him or not, but then I
didn't see why not, or what purpose it would serve either of
us if I didn't. "Did it hurt?" I asked. I remembered sticking
my fingers into the electrical outlets at home sometimes,
when I was a little kid. How much *that* had hurt. I did it
more than once, but maybe no more than three times.
You'd think it wouldn't have taken more than the once, but
I just always wondered at what point the electricity would
arrive out of those tiny little slots where it looked like nothing could be.

"Oh yes," the Electric Man told me, busying himself

again with the task of my portrait. "Oh yes, it hurt very much," he said. He picked up his tray of paints again and gazed down at the small canvas. It appeared that he did not want to talk after that, and after a quarter of an hour went by in which we didn't speak at all, I asked him if he thought one day soon I could see the portrait. He said, "I leave tomorrow, you can see it then." And then a little while later, he got up and said: "That will do."

IN THE MORNING HE was not downstairs when I did the rounds with the butter, and when I went about by the shore collecting chairs and parasols from the beach I did not see him there either—shielded, as usual, by the broad rim of his woman's straw hat.

He must have slipped out while I was down by the shore, because when I returned to the Auberge there was no one whose ice melted so fast and I spent the lazy pre-dinner hours casually refilling trays for the few guests who ate their little things very slowly and never seemed to need anything.

As usual, just before dinner, I checked my mail slot in the lobby of the Auberge, though there was rarely anything to find, and there it was: the small canvas, all wrapped up inside a rather tattered paper bag. I felt relieved—and not a little flattered. All that time, it would seem now, the painting had been just for me. But when I tore away the wrapping I saw that what he had left me was not a portrait at all, but the most banal seascape, not unlike the one outside the window of the Auberge, which the man with the hat would have seen quite clearly over my shoulder as I sat for all those hours opposite him in a straight-backed chair.

For a moment, I still hoped that he had kept the real portrait of me for himself and had given me this canvas only as a sort of substitute. But then I thought that it wasn't very likely: I had only ever seen one canvas in the little room. It seemed the man was, after all, perhaps quite literally, insane. I felt disappointed, and was about to make my way back to my room, when I noticed there was something else in the bag. It was the broad-brimmed hat, all rolled up—I hadn't imagined it could be made so small. It had a note attached to it, too, which said, in childish scrawl, *Because you're fair, like me, and must burn easily in too much sun.*

WHEN, A DAY OR TWO after that, I returned a stack of French novels to the little library that the owners kept in the Auberge's lounge, I slipped the canvas in with the books because I didn't want to look at it anymore. There was something very sad to me about the uniform blue of the ocean and the perfect little *m*'s for birds that had been drawn onto the sky. I wanted to get rid of it, but I didn't want to just throw it away.

My routine continued, unchanged by the Electric Man's absence. I made my rounds with the butter in the morning, and then went down to the beach, where I collected abandoned chairs and parasols, and then stretched out in the shade—covered head to toe so I wouldn't burn, and wearing the Electric Man's broad-brimmed hat. I still did that—still stretched out on the beach in the shade—even after I'd stopped going down to the water anymore because it was actually cold and green, or pretending to read French novels because none of the words ever seemed to hang together in a consecutive way.

I would just stare around, my hand curled to my eye sometimes, like a telescope. A strange sort—most basic sort—of telescope, of course; it never made anything appear any closer, or farther away. I never tried to summon myself, as I had done as a child. Never tried to press myself—myself as I *felt myself to be*, most truly—through the small space that was left between my farthest-away finger and the curve of my thumb. I think I didn't want to risk finding that, were I to try, I wouldn't feel that tingling, rushing electric sensation that I had when I was a child.

Someday, I thought, while I lay stretched out on an Auberge chair in the shady spot of the beach—before returning to refill the trays and pass out drinks and bills, and then drinks again, to the late-afternoon guests—I would try it again. I would try to feel myself *alive* again in the way that I had when I was very young. Perhaps the Electric Man had inspired me. To find that "blank space" of myself—or whatever it was he had said. There was no real *reason*, after all, I thought to myself, that I could not feel that way again—it was, in fact, quite possible, and someday, I thought, when I was feeling particularly well, I would try.

THEN, AT THE VERY END of August, perhaps a week or two after I had last seen the Electric Man, Madame Rondelle, the owner of the Auberge, stopped me on the stair. "I had a note from Monsieur Wyatt," she said. She always spoke to me in English, because she was no more French than me, though she spoke the language more perfectly. She was a Swede, but of course her English, as well as her French, was impeccable. I rarely saw her long enough to speak with her, though, and, in addition, she always made me nervous. She seemed so sure of herself all the time, and because I was never sure of anything, especially that summer, I always suspected that I was misunderstanding things—even in my own language. I had got that used to second-guessing.

I didn't even know who Monsieur Wyatt was, for example. "Who?" I asked.

Madame Rondelle looked up at me, sharply. "The man with the hat," she told me. "He knows *you*," she said. "He said to give you a kind hello." She hesitated then, before stepping away—evidently wanting to say something more, but for some reason uncertain. "A very *dear* man," she told me, as if that were an explanation of something. "I'm a friend of his sister. He's been coming here for years." Then she hesitated again. "A little strange," she said, and her hand left the railing where she had placed it and fluttered up to her chest, as if it hoped to retain something there. "But a very *dear* dear man," she insisted, as if that settled it. But still she did not immediately move to go, and in the space of time in which we both lingered—she on the stair, about to decide whether to finally complete her ascent, and I at the bottom, equally unsure of whether I should relieve her of the conversation, make some excuse to go—I tried to think of some perfect thing to say to her of him. But I couldn't think of anything. I didn't want to tell her about the painting, that was certain. Someday she would find it, in going through the library, and throw it out; I didn't think she should know anything of its history if that were to be the case.

"What does he do now?" I asked, for want of anything else. "I mean," I said, "how is it he has the time, and the—" I paused, "the resources, I mean, to stay?" Then I realized I'd been rude. But I wanted to know. I didn't imagine that a former member of the Bulgarian Circus would have a very large pension. I presumed, in that moment, because I had never thought of it before, that he must have been from one of those large and wealthy New England families who could afford to finance, and be responsible for, the whims—however fleeting—of their members. It was because that suddenly seemed clear to me that I thought with some shame that it would have been better for me not to have mentioned the money at all. Money was embarrassing when there was either too much or too little of it, and the means to the Electric Man's situation—which was evidently comfortable—would have been better left unspoken.

But Madame did not seem perturbed by the question. If anything she adopted a more conciliatory tone. "From what I gather," she said—she began her ascent once more as she spoke, but slowly—"he gets a fairly sizeable cheque from Veterans of Foreign Wars." It would have been difficult to say whether she had whispered or shouted the words. There seemed, anyway, to be equal attention paid to both emphasizing and concealing the information that the sentence contained. Then she shrugged. "That's what gets forwarded here," she said.

I must have looked surprised, or like I was about to say something, and I don't think that she wanted to be detained much longer. "He got wounded badly in one of the wars," she explained—as if she wished now that she hadn't brought it up at all. "I'm not sure which one, he was in so many. Sam—that's his sister, my friend—she believes"—she had almost reached the top of the stair; pretty soon she would disappear—"they pay him to keep quiet about certain things, you know, that are too—" she paused again, just slightly, just before she was lost to the upstairs of the Auberge and said, "too awful to talk about." She had another tone in her voice now, a very sad faraway note had crept in, and her hand had remained at her throat as she mounted the stair. "He used to bathe down at the shore when he first came with Sam," she said. "But for some reason, he's stopped bathing now." She looked down to where I stood—it seemed a great distance. "It used to give me quite a fright to see him," she continued. Then she made a face, and tossed her hand that had been held at her throat in the air as if whatever she'd wished to hold as she'd ascended was useless to her now. "Just—awful," she said, "his whole body all scarred over the way it was. Whatever it was that happened to him, I don't know. But I should *hope*," she said, "that he's getting, for it, a pretty compensation." With a slight nod then, which served to mark her final departure, she turned, and continued up the stairs.

The Limit

"DO YOU WANT TO DRIVE?" Daniel asks Anna. All of a sudden—he doesn't know why. As soon as he says it he wants to take it back. He wants to laugh like it was a bit of a joke that he had with himself, but then he can't because he hates the kind of man who would laugh like that, even if he is that kind of man.

Anna is thirteen, and lives in Milwaukee with her mother. Daniel hasn't seen her in eight months, and still he'd had to wrangle with Diane for weeks just to get her out here for four days. Now he wonders if he should have gone to all the trouble.

"What!" Anna says. "Now?" Now Daniel is happy that he said it. It's been over twenty minutes since he picked her up at the station but this is the first time that she seems to actually *be there*. The first time that she seems to be actually talking to *him*—and not to some cut-out version of himself, the way it had seemed to him before. Answering his questions too politely—as if she were practising for someone else.

They have just taken the last exit heading out of Sioux Falls. There is still another twenty miles before they get to the old place, where Daniel's mother still lives, even though he's been after her for years to move into town. "Sure," Daniel says. And tries to find some reason that this might be a good idea. "I was your age when I first learned," he says, finally. Even though it's not true. Then: "Why not? This ain't Milwaukee, you know. In case you hadn't noticed."

"I noticed," Anna says. But not unkindly. She looks at him, interested now. Wondering what he'll do next.

He pulls off onto the side of the road. "Here," he says. "Let's switch."

DANIEL HAD NEVER HAD any intention of being an absent dad. He wasn't the type. That was for guys who moved around a lot and couldn't commit to things. But now, *bam*. Intended or not—here it is. His daughter beside him in the car, and not a single thing to say to her. Not even anything to point out on the road as they pass. The whole goddamn state, he thinks suddenly, looks pretty much the same, if you don't get too technical. Usually, he likes it this way. Usually, he likes to get out past Sioux Falls and have the landscape suddenly fall away, as if it didn't exist anymore—likes the way that there's still some things that remain, like that, unchanged. Or at least that change so slowly that a man like him can keep up, and understand.

That is not the case with, for example, Anna, who has grown so much in the past eight months that he found himself embarrassed when he went to meet her at the train. He went forward awkwardly at first, as if maybe she wouldn't know him. As if maybe he'd have to wave his hands around to get her to notice him, and say something like, *It's me, it's your dad.* Maybe she wouldn't even want him to hug her anymore. Daniel thought about that—too late, with a little flurry of panic in his chest—when he did hug her, and his arms felt long.

It would be a shock to any man, he told himself, on the way out of town, to see his daughter tall, so suddenly, like that. To see his daughter looking suddenly like the sort of daughters other men had. Who snapped their gum, and wore lip gloss, and had breasts. There was supposed to be a progression toward these sorts of things.

THEY ARE ONLY ABOUT seven miles from the Knutsen farm when Daniel pulls the car over. They can already see it, even from that distance. Or what's left of it. A couple of years back the place was sold to a local developer and pretty much flattened—but Daniel always forgets. He always expects to see it anyway. For the tree line to appear on the horizon in the old, familiar way. But then it doesn't.

Once, the trees had been so thick the Knutsens had lost an entire herd of buffalo to them. They'd got separated up inside the woods and couldn't find their way out again. The police and the fire department had to be called—just to get rid of them. It's funny to think about that now. About how the buffalo had stood around all night, shivering in woods that don't even exist anymore. Even so, Daniel keeps expecting them. Right up to the last moment when he passes the raked gravel lot where the old farmhouse used to be.

That had been the year Daniel was eleven. In fact, it was the afternoon of his eleventh birthday—after Daniel had had his presents, but before the birthday cake—that his father picked up the phone when it rang and said into it, "I could have seen *this* coming." The buffalo had been at the Knutsen farm for only a month. Less—his mother said—if you calculated all the time that it took to get them out of the truck and into the pen. Which was pretty much forever. A full day, anyway, that's how long it took old Mr. Knutsen, and the six Knutsen boys, and the tractor trailer man, to get those buffalo where they were going. They just didn't want to get out of the truck. And then, of course, once they were out and into the pen, they didn't want to stay there. The morning Daniel turned eleven they bust up the fence the Knutsen boys had spent all spring fixing, and that was pretty much the end of the buffalo.

A month before, when the buffalo first arrived, Daniel's father had said, "Those Knutsens, you got to hand it to them—they got an eye to the future." But when the buffalo got out and all hell broke loose, he said, "I could have seen it a mile away." Daniel didn't say anything. His father seemed so confident that he had known *from the beginning* how things would go now that they had actually *happened* that Daniel thought his saying that before about the "eye to the future" had only been a kind of a joke. Daniel was just beginning to realize that adults did that sometimes— said things they didn't mean. And it wasn't because they couldn't think of the right way to say what they meant—

they probably could. It was just what they did. Sometimes they even said the very opposite of what they meant, and liked it that way. They thought it was funny, and that whatever it was they said wasn't meant to be taken seriously anyhow. Hardly anything that grown-up people said, Daniel was beginning to realize, was meant to be serious.

Any way you looked at it, though, the Knutsens were forward thinking—everyone admitted that. This was unusual—especially in those days—in their postage-stamp-sized corner of the world. It had been a surprise to Daniel the first time he looked at the state of South Dakota on a map and saw the way that it could be made to look so small—the exact size and shape of a postage stamp. Whenever he got outside, and wandered around, like his mother was always bugging him to do, everything always seemed so big. Even his own tiny corner of that other tiny corner of . . . but when he started thinking about it, it made his head hurt, and he had to stop before he ever got anywhere near to thinking about the entire state of South Dakota. It seemed that everything just went on and on forever, because even if he ever got to be able to think about South Dakota, that would be only the beginning of thinking about everything else.

Once, he told his mother about trying to think about that. He said: "I start off real small, and then I try to think up, bigger and bigger, as slowly as I can, but then my mind gets fuzzy and I can't think anymore. How come?" His mother had laughed—but in a nice way that wasn't really directed at him, and which Daniel always found vaguely comforting. "You just can't think about those things, honey," she told him. "You'll find out there's a lot of things like that."

It wasn't the answer he'd been looking for, and maybe it was because he could always get a yes from his dad when he couldn't from his mother, and the other way around, that he believed that, in this case, too, if he wanted a different answer he'd just have to keep looking.

DANIEL EASES THE GEARSHIFT into Drive. His hand is over-top of Anna's and, once the stick has clicked in at *D*, he says, "Now just step on the gas, just a little, just a little." Anna doesn't step on the gas. His hand is still on hers, and underneath that is the gearshift. "Which one's the gas?" she says. Daniel tells her which one, and they lurch forward, going too fast, and then a second later they stop entirely, with a bounce. "Okay, okay," Daniel says. Anna looks like she might cry. One of her eyebrows is all knit up and she's got a hold of her top lip with her bottom teeth. "Okay," Daniel says, "that's okay. Try again, just ease the gas on, and don't get scared." He's taken his hand off the gearshift and has put it on the wheel, just above where her right hand is knotted around the rim.

"Are you sure about this?" she says. That look on her face.

"No," Daniel jokes. "I'm not sure about anything." And he laughs a little, but she doesn't, and then he feels stupid. "Except that"—he tries to rescue himself from the joke— "for the next five minutes, even with you at the wheel, we're going to be ab-so-lute-ly fine." He taps the rhythm of the word *absolutely* out on her hand on the wheel, which is gripped very tightly. Then he adds "kiddo"—after the fact. It was something that he used to call her. Not too long ago, though it must seem like a long time ago to her. He hasn't used the word on her yet this visit, and isn't sure, even as he says it, that he should. It's okay, though, when he says it. It comes out okay.

This time the car starts more smoothly. Daniel thinks with some surprise how easy it is to forget how many things get learned—and so quickly. Simple things. Like driving. Like riding a bike, or tying your shoes. Even that used to be a real *effort*, he remembers. How he had got it wrong so often, and how his father had shown him, taking his hands in his own, again and again.

That was why he'd wanted a kid in the first place. Even when he was a kid himself, he'd always thought it would be nice to have someone, like that, to *show* things to. To say, *Look, here's how it works. I'll show you.*

THE DAY THE BUFFALO ARRIVED, Daniel's mother and her friend Cheryl, who worked at the meat-processing plant off the main highway, took Daniel to watch them be unloaded at the Knutsens' farm. Cheryl had delicate fingers and her nails were long and narrow at the tips. They were always a different colour each time Daniel saw them. When the buffalo came, and they went to watch, Cheryl kept her hands on the steering wheel, and he could see them from his position in the back seat. Sometimes she lit a cigarette, and he watched the way she did it. It seemed more complicated, and therefore more beautiful, when she did it, because her nails made everything seem difficult, and out of reach. Cheryl's hands were different from his mother's hands. It wasn't that his mother's hands weren't nice—they were. It was just that they were—hands. With short pale nails, and medium-sized fingers. Cheryl's hands didn't look like hands at all—or if they did, they looked like they were meant to belong to someone else, who didn't live where they lived, or didn't work at the meat-processing plant near town. Once he'd heard his father say, "With those hands you oughta be a secretary or something, Cheryl—show 'em off," and his mother had got mad and said, "She ought to be more than a *secretary*," but then she didn't say anything else, or suggest what "more than a secretary" might be, which was something that Daniel, and maybe even his mother, didn't know.

Cheryl parked the car just a little ways up the road, at some distance from the house, and then she and Daniel and his mother sat there for most of an hour and waited. For a long time nothing happened. They saw all the Knutsen boys running around in circles in the yard. There was hollering, but they couldn't tell what was being said because they were still some distance from the place, and they had the windows shut tight. His mother smoked a cigarette, which was something he'd never seen her do before, and the car filled up with so much smoke that his eyes stung.

But he liked it that way. The way the smoke fogged every-thing up so that it seemed like a long distance between the front and the back seat. Like there was all sorts of room suddenly for things to take place in, if they were going to.

Finally, Cheryl turned around to look at him, his face smeared up against the glass. He had got bored of watch-ing the Knutsen boys run around, and didn't believe in the buffalo anymore, so was not even really looking out of the window at all. Instead, he was just sort of staring ahead, trying to keep his eyes open without blinking for long per-iods of time, which made his eyes sting even worse. When they'd been open for a particularly long time he discov-ered that he could make them unfocus pretty easily, which made the world go all blurry. So he concentrated on doing that—on getting his eyes to unfocus, and then, quick as he could, he'd focus them in again. Focus, unfocus, focus, unfocus, his eyes went—but to Cheryl when she turned around it probably just looked like he was doing nothing, just staring off into space.

"Let's take this kid home," Cheryl said, and his mom looked back at him then too, and said, "You had enough, sweetie?" As if the buffalo had been his idea.

Later that day, Daniel's father got the word that the Knutsens had finally got their buffalo unloaded into the field. He hung up the phone and said, "Well, we got some new neighbours, ladies." Daniel's mother and Cheryl were sitting on the couch, their feet tucked up under them, drinking something with ice, which clinked in the glass.

"Damn," said Cheryl, "I would have liked to see them all charge out of there."

And then not a month later, Daniel's father was on the phone again, before the birthday cake, only this time he had a different look on his face, saying, "I could have seen it coming a mile away." Or maybe it was "I should have— I *should've* seen it coming"—maybe that's what he'd said when he hung up the phone.

"Don't anyone go outside," Daniel's father had instructed them then. He seemed to like the way that sounded: the words alarming, but the voice in itself composed, and calm. "We got twenty mad buffalo storming around out there. I want everyone to stay put till we get all this taken care of," he said. Then he went out to the shed and came back with his rifle. His mother sat with Daniel at the kitchen table, where he'd been doing some homework, and she had been looking through a magazine, and helping him from time to time when he ran into problems with long division.

"Oh dear," she'd said, when his father first went out, "I don't like the sounds of this." Then she got up and used the telephone herself, and Daniel heard her giggle a little into the phone in the other room—she was probably talking to Cheryl—but in that way she had sometimes, when she didn't mean to be giggling.

By the time Daniel's father had got back, she was sitting at the table again, reading her magazine. She and Daniel looked up when he came in, and he seemed to remember something then, and put down the rifle, and went back outside. He'd leaned the rifle up against Daniel's mother's chair, which was closest to the door, and it looked silly to see it like that, next to his mother.

When his father came back he was carrying another gun, and he said to Daniel, "Daniel you can come too," and then he extended his hand out with the gun in it, so that Daniel was supposed to get out of his chair and walk over to his father, and take up the gun.

He had shot a gun before. Many times. His father had taught him, and by now he had been out with his father for two deer-hunting seasons in a row, although technically he was supposed to wait until he was twelve. Sometimes his father had gone out for grouse with him, too, but he had still shot only in practice and never for real, even when his father had purposely held back on a shot he could have taken, and said, "This one's yours, son." He would always just come up with some reason that it hadn't made sense to fire, but he didn't know why he did that, every time. It wasn't because he didn't want to kill the bird. He wanted to kill the bird more than anything.

"Oh, come on, don't," Daniel's mother said, when Daniel got up to take the gun from his father, and put on his boots, and follow him out to the truck. "This is not messing around, you know. I thought you just told us both to stay inside. That seemed like a plan to me."

"You stay in," Daniel's father said, and went out, so that Daniel had to shove his boots on quickly to not get left behind. His feet weren't all the way down into the boots when he started for the door, so they made him walk funny. His mother had got up and moved out onto the porch in her slippers. She was probably cold.

"You be careful," she said, when Daniel waddled past with his feet not in his shoes, and his gun in one hand, outstretched, away from his body. "You be careful with my son," she yelled, a little louder than she needed to, for his father to hear.

THEY DRIVE FOR ABOUT three minutes, very slowly. Anna is concentrating hard on the road, and has her jaw set tight, her hands all tensed up on the wheel. Daniel lets go of the wheel after a while himself, and then watches her— frozen like that, not a muscle in her body moving—and yet moving—the outside world passing steadily. He digs back in his memory for some brief moment that would show him how all of this was inevitable in some way; that this was the way it was supposed to be with them. Some brief memory. Anything. From when Anna was small. If he can think of one thing, he will certainly share it with her, and then she will see the way he has always known her. And still knows her. And will.

But he can't think anything.

Then, after about three minutes are up, Anna pulls the car expertly off to the side of the road, and puts on the brake. "I'm done," she says.

"But you're doing so well!" Daniel says. He brings his hand down briefly on her arm, which is off the steering wheel now, and lying in her lap. The movement is intended to be conciliatory, but it comes off more as a bit of a slap.

"*You* drive," Anna says, as if it were a disgusting thing to do. "It's *your* car."

Too late, Daniel realizes he has made a large, and irrevocable, error.

"Okay," he says, quietly. "I will."

ON THE MAIN HIGHWAY, their guns on the rack at the top of the cab, Daniel felt happy in a way that he had not imagined he would when his father came back from the shed that second time with the gun. His father's dog, Sugar, was sitting in between them, peering eagerly ahead, out the front glass. Sugar went everywhere with his father. It was the usual thing to see his father returning from wherever he went with Sugar racing beside him down the drive. About a mile from home, where the road split and one way went in a loop back to the highway, and the other went to their house, Daniel's father always let her out of the cab and she'd run the rest of the way home. She could keep up, mostly—when Daniel's father didn't tease her and drive too fast. Once, his father had said to Daniel—when Daniel was driving back home with him and Sugar and they'd stopped to let Sugar leap out, and race off, getting a head start on them—"Sometimes, I wish I could let myself out and run around beside myself for a while, I get to feeling so restless. You ever get like that?"

Daniel had said no, because he wasn't positive that he

knew what his father meant, and didn't want to have to back something up that he'd made a mistake about. He did *think* he knew what his father was talking about though, and he was surprised because he'd thought that only small boys and not grown-up men felt that way.

Long before they got there, they could already see how packed the Knutsen place was. There were even a couple of police cars and a fire truck lined up along the side of the road so that Daniel's father had to park some distance away, though not as far as Cheryl and his mother had parked. They walked, from that distance, up to the main drive, where some of the Knutsen boys and a couple of police officers were standing around. Daniel found that, without trying particularly, he could match his father's stride. They were crunching along on the gravel shoulder, their feet falling in unison, so that the sound they made was like one man walking, instead of a man and a boy.

His father talked to a police officer for a moment, and spelled out his name, which the officer wrote down, then they headed across the field in the direction of the woods. They could see the men at various stages of nearness to the tree line, which was a good mile or so away. Some had started off just minutes before, and so were up close, still large and distinct. He could still hear their voices, some of them. Others were almost to the edge of the woods, about to disappear. The rest were somewhere in between.

While his father had been talking to the sheriff, Daniel saw Cheryl come out of the barn, smoking a cigarette. She was talking to one of the Knutsen boys and looked upset. Everyone looked upset; it shouldn't have surprised him that Cheryl might too. But it did. He wondered what Cheryl was doing talking to a Knutsen, and then he thought it was interesting that it had never crossed his mind that Cheryl got sad sometimes, or that she knew anybody else besides his mother and him. He tried to catch her eye when she came out of the barn, but she wasn't looking at him. Her head was bent down into the collar of her big man's jacket and she looked kind of swallowed up in a way that all of a sudden made Daniel not want to talk to her anymore.

They had started out across the field. At first, Daniel's father had his hand on Daniel's shoulder, and then it was off. Sometimes, Daniel's boots got sucked into the mud where the ground was soft, and then he'd have to stop for a half second to squelch them out, and in that short time he'd fall behind his father and then have to double step to catch back up again. His father didn't speak to him until they got to the edge of the wood and then he said, "You stick close to me. You're not worried, are you? You can go on back, you know." But Daniel shook his head. He wasn't worried. In fact, he had never felt so free of worry. It was like he had let himself out to run around somewhere. He felt that light, and empty inside, but at the same time as if for the first time he knew exactly who he was—the precise limits of his body—and what to do.

Daniel's father nodded, and they entered the wood.

For a long time they wandered in what seemed like circles. After a while it occurred to Daniel that they might be lost, but then he didn't think they were. His mind drifted near the idea and then away, as if it too had begun to wander in circles. He no longer felt light or empty in the way that he had before. He had, he realized—uncomfortable and wet-footed—been returned to his body, and from that position could no longer detect relative distances—or the point at which one thing, like himself, ended or began. His feet had been rubbing for some time against the wet wool of his socks inside his boots, he noticed that now—he would not be surprised if a raw sore had already developed there. It was at the precise moment that he noticed that, that two things happened: the gun, which had until that point felt like an extension of himself, felt suddenly heavy in his hand, and he saw the buffalo.

It was bigger than he could have imagined, having only seen them from a diminishing distance.

"Shit," Daniel's father said when, in another moment, he saw it, too. He grabbed at the hood of Daniel's jacket and kind of tugged at it. Daniel got down on the ground like it was a movie and they were the ones being shot at. "No, *get up*," Daniel's father hissed at him. "Back up, back up." He had his gun raised and he was shooing Daniel behind him with one hand. The buffalo did not see them, but was standing looking off into the closely grown wood as if at nothing.

"I got'm, I got'm," Daniel's father said, and then the gun went off and the buffalo was gone.

Daniel realized that he had tightly shut his eyes and that was why there had been no progression. One minute he had seen the buffalo looking off into the woods, and then there was no buffalo at all. The trees were so closely grown that it seemed impossible that an animal so large could have squeezed through them and disappeared.

Daniel sensed his father's disappointment, although neither of them said anything. When the buffalo was gone, Daniel's father simply took down his gun, wiped off the muzzle, and then turned in the direction that Daniel was, without looking at him. "Come on," he said. "Which way?" Daniel didn't know what to say. He hadn't seen the direction that the buffalo had gone, and then he wasn't even that sure if they should be running after it or away from it. He pointed straight ahead, and his father took off in the direction that he pointed.

When Daniel and his father got back home that evening they left the rifles on the rack because neither of them wanted to put them away. It would have seemed to be too outright an admission that it was over—that they wouldn't go looking for buffalo again. The next day they both had work or school, and probably by that time anyway, the police and the fire department would have the situation under control and they wouldn't need volunteers anymore.

Daniel's mother was scrubbing the bathroom when they got back in, and didn't rush up to greet them as he'd thought she might.

"Catch a buffalo?" she said when they got in the door,

in a voice that Daniel recognized as one that was capable of starting up a fight between her and his father.

"Nope," Daniel's father said.

"Too bad," Daniel's mother said.

"Yep, I sure wouldn't have minded having a buffalo to eat off of all winter, and neither would've you and neither would've Daniel."

"Knutsen's buffalo," Daniel's mother corrected him.

"Not if I shot it," Daniel's father said. "Not if Daniel here shot it. That was the deal. Anyone could have had himself a buffalo tonight."

"Too bad," Daniel's mother said again, in that voice.

"Yep," Daniel's father agreed. He gave Daniel a wink, and then wondered aloud what they were having for dinner if it wasn't anything wild.

Later that evening Daniel went walking down the road toward the direction of the Knutsens' farm. He wasn't planning on going as far as that. He wasn't supposed to be out at all. But his mother and father were both in the back room watching TV and not paying him any attention, so he'd just slipped out. The night was cool and calm. It was like walking through a picture of another planet. The air was that still—stopped, almost. He felt like he could walk on and on forever in that air, that it would offer no resistance—and that would be the good, and really the only, choice that he could make in his life. But then he thought about his parents. About how worried they would be for him, out there with the buffalo, if they realized he was gone. Reluctantly, he turned and walked back to the house.

But then, when he entered the house, he found that too was good. He found that too had been a fine decision—and he saw very clearly in that moment that he would never know what the right thing would be to do in his life.

WHEN HE IS DRIVING AGAIN, Daniel tries to change the subject. He racks his brain for a subject that might interest Anna, but she is sullen with him now, and refuses to elaborate on any of the answers she supplies to the questions he asks. All her answers come out sounding like he is a fool to have to ask in the first place, as if of course there would be only one answer to *that*, and everyone would know it but him. Actually, he feels that way.

They aren't far now. In another mile or so, past where the Knutsen farm used to be, they will reach the junction and choose the road to the right. This will lead them to the old place, where Daniel's mother still lives. Maybe Daniel will tell Anna about how his father used to let Sugar off right there, to run. That, at least, would be something to say.

He wishes that Anna wasn't in such a rotten mood, it's putting him in one too. But it's not her fault. He shouldn't have made her drive.

What he really wishes is that they—he and his daughter— could arrive at his mother's house happy and laughing, as if they were the most natural companions in the world—

which they were. Which they were *supposed* to have been. His mother would see, then, that although some things had come to pass that Daniel himself or anyone else could not have foreseen—everything was going on anyway. In another way. Equally good.

Failing that, what Daniel wishes is that at least they were back at the beginning of the drive and Anna was polite to him again.

The junction seems a long while to wait before he says anything again, so he says, "Whatcha thinking about, honey?"

He tries to make his voice sound cheerful and light, as if the question has come out of nowhere and isn't attached to anything else—even to any anticipation of reply.

Anna says, *"Nothing,"* and Daniel knows that he has made another mistake. After that he doesn't say anything for a moment, but then he feels reckless. He feels that maybe he doesn't even care anymore. He thinks, *What the hell, I'm just going to say any old thing, whatever I feel like,* and half turns to Anna and says, "I've always found that to be difficult."

Anna ignores him, or perhaps she hasn't even heard. Daniel keeps going anyway. "I mean I've tried," he says. "It's not that I haven't tried. But I just can never quite do it. So, if *you* can," he tells her, and by now his words are coming out a little faster and hard. He feels like a fool, and wishes he could just quit talking. Instead he shrugs. "Well," he says—to wrap up—"I guess that's pretty cool for you."

Anna is still ignoring him, but she doesn't look quite so angry now. Maybe it's just Daniel's imagination, but it occurs to him that he may have, now, the smallest of chances, so he tries again. "Are you *really* thinking of nothing?" he asks, and now he lets a teasing note creep into his voice. If he can get her to laugh before he gets to his mother's place, then everything will be all right. Eight months ago he could have done it. He remembers that about Anna, certainly. She'd never been good at holding a grudge. She'd get upset, enough to frighten him sometimes, but then—in a moment—she'd be happy again, just like that, as if those small frustrations, which had somehow got so out of hand, had never existed at all.

"I mean *really* really," Daniel tries again. He smiles as he says it in her direction—to where she is looking out the window, at the approaching junction. In another second, without turning her head, she will be staring right down the road that they will turn down toward home. That is the way it is when you are travelling, even at a moderate pace, in a moving vehicle. What will she think then? Daniel wonders this but knows, even as he wonders it, that it is something he will never ask.

That is the pace they are travelling at. Daniel gets four words into the distance between the approach and the turn, and then he wonders how many more he can get in before his mother's house. If the space between here and the house is enough. "I mean right now," he says. "Are you thinking nothing . . . *now?*" He waits. "How about," and pauses again, "now!" he says, very quickly and loud. Maybe she even jumps a little.

Before she smiles Daniel sees it. "Hey?" he asks. Encouraged. "Hey? Hey?" He says again, and takes a risk, and touches her. He takes a hand off the wheel and gives her a little poke on the shoulder to match his last "hey?"

She sways a little toward the window, but doesn't pull back from his touch, as he'd been afraid that she might. And she does, she smiles. At first she tries to hide it, but then she shifts in her seat, and tosses her hair over her shoulder to look at him—at Daniel—and then he can see that everything's all right.

"I didn't think so," Daniel says, to answer his own question.

Once they make the turn, leaving what's left of the Knutsen place behind, the land really does seem to just fall away. It doesn't drop off, it just extends itself out—just stretches on and off, right out onto blankness. Especially this time of year, when all the colours are so muted and not even really colours at all but just a suggestion of the sort of colour they once had been. It just seems to go on for what, Daniel assumes, is as good as forever.

He thinks this, and then feels happy that he does. Happy, too, when he realizes he has chosen to stay out here, in this part of the world, when it was not at all certain that that is what he would do. That he has chosen to stay in the Midwest, where a man can think thoughts like the one he has thought, just now, seems to him like the best kind of decision he could have made. He knows that on the East Coast and on the West, there is the imposition, always, of objects on other objects. The sky is interrupted by the hills, the hills by the trees, the trees by more hills, and houses, and so on. But out here, in the middle, it's possible to find a section of the road to look out at and not see anything for miles. It is possible just to see and see until it gets hazy and you can't see anymore—and even at that point, at the point where you stop being able to see any longer, it's not because what's out there is covered up by anything, it's just—that's the limit.

FRENCH LESSONS

*Thereupon, the signifier (the third meaning)
is not filled; it keeps in a permanent state
of depletion (a term from linguistics that
designates the empty, all-purpose verbs—
for example, the verb faire). We might also
say, on the other hand—and this would be
quite as true—that this same signifier is not
empty (cannot empty itself); it maintains a
state of perpetual erethism, desire not finding issue in that spasm of the signified that
normally causes the subject to sink voluptu-
ously back into the peace of nominations.*

—ROLAND BARTHES

For Sarah

WHEN MARTHA FIRST arrived in Paris—before she met Charlie, and settled down, and her real life began—she stayed with blind old Madame Bernard on the Left Bank, in an old apartment with narrow rooms, which linked themselves like train cars all the way back. Madame took her coffee in bed, and at exactly 8 a.m. Martha would fix it and carry it in, to where Madame, already raised on her pillows, would be reading books in Braille, her fingers skimming the surface of the page, making a whistling noise. If not for the morning coffee, Martha perhaps never would have been hired at all, because that was, very nearly, the extent of her duties for the day. She tidied the place, but more or less of her own accord, and sometimes she wondered if Madame would even notice if she let things go. This was absurd, of course—Madame noticed everything.

She would get up and dress herself without assistance— often wearing the same chemise that she'd slept in, along with a pair of trousers belonging to the professor (her husband, by then deceased), which she rolled to the knee. Then she listened to Wagner, placing the needle mid-record herself and allowing the aria to play through, at least several times. It was always the same: "Erda's Warning," from scene 4 of *Das Rheingold*. Initially it had agitated Martha to begin every morning in this way, but she grew used to it quickly, and after a while even began to look forward to the ritual. Within a single month she could replay the exact progression of the scene in her head and found herself doing so on occasion—sometimes long after she'd left Madame and Madame's apartment behind. Which she did, less than a year later. Arriving at Charlie's smaller, sunnier apartment in the Eleventh, with the French doors (it had seemed, when she'd visited Charlie and fallen in love, that it was for those doors, and not for Paris—or for Charlie—that she'd come), she found her mornings without the Wagner rather quiet.

Madame also insisted, despite Martha's repeated efforts, on assembling her own meals, which consisted of three long baguette sandwiches, for which Martha purchased the bread each morning. The cheese she bought according to the specific request of Madame from a vendor at the Thursday market who had been described in such unfaultable detail that she'd spotted him immediately, still several stalls away. She'd noticed his hair first, half curly, and then the way that his forehead sloped and completed itself—*"à ne pas manquer"*—in a long and narrow nose.

Once, at the beginning of her stay, Martha—having helped herself generously to the cheese—replaced it midweek with one from a Saturday market farther along the boulevard. This cheese had looked and smelled, to Martha, just the same, and she had hoped (knowing, truly, nothing then) that it *was*. Madame Bernard, however, had frowned when opening the package and, with a polite sniff, asked Martha to refrain in the future from *les jeux* when it came to *les fromages*. Martha's French was still so poor that at first she assumed Madame was objecting to her *jupes*—the short skirts she wore in those days—until she remembered that Madame was blind.

Meals for Martha were to be included in the arrangement that she and Madame Bernard had agreed upon, but on her arrival nothing was provided and no mention of an alternative plan made. She walked by the fruit stands on market days, her eyes lingering on the apples and bananas and pears; but never once did she afford herself the luxury of purchasing anything. One Thursday, however, before leaving for the market, she worked up the courage to request a little extra money, with which she might buy a few items of her own. Madame was positioned comfortably in her favourite chair, reading in the dark, as she always did in the late afternoon. (It never failed to surprise Martha to come across her that way: in the near blackness, a book open on her knee.)

Madame did not look up as Martha approached—nor as, in elliptical sentences that looped back on themselves and led ultimately nowhere, she commenced her stumbling appeal. Not once did Madame interrupt, or offer anything—some predicate, some verb—into the silences that sometimes ensued. (It was within these silences that Martha seemed almost to live in those days, as though she imagined that the words she did not yet know dwelt there, too, and so there she hunted for them—lucklessly.)

At last, when in a final and lingering hesitation Madame understood that Martha's request was complete, she removed her finger from the page, laid the book aside, and shuffled to the kitchen without a word—her rolled-up trousers rustling at the knee. Reaching up to the high shelf above the stove, she chose from among the other crowded objects a bowl of waxen fruit, which she offered to Martha, evidently pleased to honour her request. The fruit glinted, still shiny in places, in the light of the kitchen's single bulb. Martha's French was indeed so poor in those days that she would have found it nearly impossible to refuse—or to clarify her request in any way—so she accepted the fruit graciously, with a nod and a smile.

Especially in moments such as these, and with Madame there were many, Martha's progress in the language struck her as frustratingly slow. She was unable to concentrate on the verb charts and vocabulary words that she had posted on her bedroom walls, and so rarely studied them at all. Instead, she drifted off into a disturbed sleep, where her dreams, laboriously translated from the English, exhausted her and she woke up tired.

IT WAS NOT UNTIL THE third month of her stay, long after the incident with the fruit, that she realized suddenly, and with what seemed like no progression toward it, that she understood; she hardly needed to concentrate anymore. She was relieved, but at the same time—and this she never would have anticipated—a little disappointed, too. It was a different sort of Paris that she'd lived in when she'd understood so little. It had been like an object. Something she could *put on*, or *examine*, or *hold*. Only once that was gone did she realize how easy it was, even in Paris, to slip into the ordinary, to begin the inevitable depreciation of things.

She would long remember the last—great—misunderstanding, however. It took place during her sixth week in the apartment, when Madame told Martha about the death of her son. The details would always remain distorted and vague, just in the way that Martha had first received them. She found herself afterward wondering about him not infrequently, sometimes horrified by small things—a desk, a globe, a knife—fearing they might have come into play somehow in a story that she had so thoroughly failed to understand.

Later, Martha would tell Ginny of the event: "I thought I had it right. You know, you can't just nod and smile with Madame, like with everyone else. I had to figure it out, you see. Where all the funny bits were, and laugh. And then, when the story got sad, I had to *know* that it did. And I did. I said 'aah' and 'oh' in all the right places, I'm sure of it! But"—and here Martha rang her hand down flat on the table, making Ginny (who for some time already had sensed the punch line) smile—"I could have *sworn*," Martha said, "that we were well *out* of the sad bits." She paused. "It's true, all stories have got to have both, but it just isn't fair when you aren't clear about which one is which."

"And so?" Ginny said, still grinning. "What happened?"

"I laughed," Martha said. "Right there, at the saddest part of the story."

This was just the punchline that Ginny had expected, and she herself laughed uproariously, which pleased Martha because she and Ginny had only just met, and it's nice to make someone you've just met laugh. Also, this was a few weeks after she'd first met Charlie, and she would have been hard pressed, then, to believe that there was really anything sad about life after all.

MADAME DID HAVE THE curious habit of pausing after she'd told a good joke, as though testing Martha to see how much—if anything—she'd understood; and Martha had learned, or thought she had, to identify those moments—to fill them in—even when she had, indeed, understood very little. On the occasion in question Madame had paused in just this way, and it was into that pause that Martha had (after a troubling moment of uncertainty) *laughed*. She knew in an instant that it was wrong, but—and for a reason that afterward she could not explain to either Ginny or herself—she did not stop laughing right away. Perhaps she hoped to suggest, in continuing to laugh, a more complete and impenetrable misunderstanding.

When she did stop, she saw that Madame's face was

stricken and sad, but not knowing what else to do—how to go backward and undo anything that had now been done— she only apologized, throwing up her hands. Then—unable to express anything in the past tense, and so refer to the misunderstanding in particular—she said, "I never understand anything," and quickly exited the room.

Nothing else passed between them until the next morning, when Martha, as usual, brought Madame her coffee in bed. As she entered the room, Madame gestured to a picture on the nightstand of a young man, then put her hand to her open mouth, pointing her forefinger to the back of her throat like the barrel of a gun, and fired.

This, Martha understood. She stopped, frozen, with the tray in her hands and did not move until Madame, who seemed afterward her usual self, plumped up her pillow and asked for her coffee, because it had not come.

IT WAS TRUE: if Martha at that time believed anything at all, it was that life, though sad in moments, sad in parts, was not—in sum—sad at all, and that the sad parts served in the end only to strengthen the overall story. Still, until she moved away from the Left Bank and into Charlie's apartment in the Eleventh, leaving Madame and Madame's son forever behind, she came to avoid certain objects, certain corners of the house. Sometimes she would find herself thinking bitterly of Madame because of the manner in which she had introduced her son—that other, perpetually doomed presence—into the house, as if he, too, were a necessary element in an otherwise essentially agreeable system of which Martha had been part. (Wagner in the mornings, cheese at noon, a mutual understanding of the perfect falsity of language.) Until, that is, Martha discovered Charlie's French doors and moved across the river and began—slowly at first—her own depreciation.

Perhaps that was the real purpose of Martha's stay with Madame Bernard. Not to provide the one luxury Madame afforded herself, the morning coffee in bed, but rather to abet a distribution of the terrible, untranslatable loneliness of that house—to share in the weight of it, and even take a little with her when she went away.

Later, she couldn't help wondering if the boy had really done it like that (Madame's forefinger, aimed at her throat), or if perhaps it had been performed somewhat differently, or even not at all, but that Madame could think—at that time—of only one foolproof method by which so great a sadness might be explained, or conveyed.

THIS WILL BE DIFFICULT TO EXPLAIN

For Monika

AN OFFICER, IN THE very early morning, came to our door. We couldn't sleep, and so we crowded on the stairs. We listened to our parents' voices: rising.

Then the officer went away, but still we didn't sleep.

My mother took the dog out to the yard. He howled and would not stop. It was dawn; the dew was on the grass. I could see it on the edges of each blade, from the door.

The officer was a small man. No bigger than my thumb. When I sat with my brother at the top of the stairs, I could, with the tip of it, conceal him entirely. I showed my brother. He laughed. Then came the shot. I covered his ears.

WHEN THE SUN CAME in it was like the moon that we were waking upon. Where was the bed? Where, finally—had I slept—I would have drifted to sleep. Everything was bare. The whole house was bare. Not one stick of furniture was left in the house.

Inside my body, I was as bare. My brother cried. I hit him. I said: Don't you cry. We're the men of this house.

He said: Where's Nino? Which was the dog. I took him to look. He was stretched on the lawn. The dew was in small and perfect beads that still clung to the grass.

There must have been, after all, some hours in which I'd slept, because in that time the world had changed and I wasn't aware of its changing.

I did not think, though, that I slept. I could have—each minute—accounted for its passing. I'd shut my eyes. I'd opened them. It was as if it were the moon that I'd opened them upon.

Perhaps I didn't sleep at all. Perhaps I've not slept my whole life since.

My mother brought one hand to her chest, and touched her heart, and held it there: We must keep still, she said. We must make very little noise. My brother's mouth she covered with the back-side of her hand.

WHEN MY FATHER'S DRUNK three beer, this is the story that he tells. My aunt Emira rolls her eyes and makes a sound through her nose. She says, waving her hand in my father's direction but speaking to us: "You know your oma."

Then she looks across the table, directly. To my brother, and to me, and ignores my father, who, again, begins the story. "In the very early morning . . ." my father says.

"She couldn't hurt a fly."

We are eating Christmas dinner. It is March.

My father's insistent, but Aunt Emira shakes her head.

"She could not have shot the dog," she says. "Listen, I was older."

When my father's drunk four beer he talks like Emira— like a German. Ordinarily, his accent's unpronounced, and he can speak in flat Canadian, and no one can tell. But after four beer. "I showed our brother," he says. "I took him to the yard. There was dew on the ground. We didn't have shoes."

By the time my father's drunk six beer, his accent is thick. "I remember Nino," he says. "It was, for him, as if it were a lazy afternoon. The way he stretched out on the lawn, as though resting."

Ten beer and my father lets some German words slip in. "I remember it exactly," he says. "*Irre!* I could—each moment—account for its passing."

Aunt Emira looks at the ceiling. My father continues: "Inside," he says, "the house was empty. A shell. Our mother put her hand up to our little brother's face, and covered it entirely."

"You fool," my aunt says. "You lunatic—fool." She gets up from her seat and slaps my father's head so it falls forward to the table and stays down.

"'Not a stick of furniture in the house,' the man says. Does that sound right?" She stands, now, above my father— above the slope of his bent neck—and glares down that grade, to the level of the board. "That they took every stick, while we slept? What use would they have had," she asks, throwing her hands in the air, "of our cheap little things?"

At twelve beer, my father's voice, again, shifts. This time to an accent that was—until my aunt came to stay with my father—unidentifiable to my brother and me. We thought it was his own invention. A strange dialect that preceded a thirteen-hour sleep. But then my aunt said once: "Sasa, now you sound like our father. You sound like a Croat. How do you do that? You were too young, and didn't even speak properly then."

My father said, "So now you must believe me. That I remember things."

"You're a drunk," my aunt said. "You're a fool. You've turned yourself into a baby again. That's how come you remember so well."

MY GRANDFATHER BUILT bridges for the SS in the war. He was not a German. "They took your father," my aunt says, and laughs sometimes when she says it, though she does not sound glad. "You drunk bastard," she says. "They took your father and you say, 'They took the bed.' They shot your uncle, and you say, 'My mother went and shot our little dog.'"

When they came again, my father's father went.

SOMETIMES MY FATHER sings us songs in German. He sings and sings until my aunt beats him with a spoon that she takes from a drawer.

It is always the same, the spoon that she chooses. I couldn't say why.

ONE DAY MY FATHER took us for a ride. He was drunk. It was my brother in the back seat and me in the front. These were the back roads around Red Deer, where we lived. Now my mother and brother and I live in town.

My father was building a hotel on our property. He said that once it was built we'd be rich. People would come, he said, from all over the world to stay in a place that was built, so carefully, by hand.

That day he said, "Come on, I'll show you where the hotel's gonna be." We said: "The hotel's in our backyard."

"Nope," said my father. "Not anymore. There's a problem with this place. It's on the flats. We'll bring it up higher. There'll be a view," my father told us. "Then people will stay."

We drove forty minutes out of town and turned up a rutted dirt track with a sign on a post by the road saying, For Sale, For Lease. The truck bumped and stuck. My father gunned the engine and swore, in German. Already he was mixing his German words in. My brother gave me a shove on the back of my neck from behind. "We'll walk," my father said, so we got out of the truck and walked up the road, which stopped short in a thicket of trees. "Here it is," he said, and spun in a circle with his arms stretched out and his hands flat.

"There's no view," my brother said. He was tired, and angry at my father for already mixing his German words in.

"Not yet," my father said. "You have to imagine. It will be like—we'll cut down the trees."

There was a T-shirt stuck on the upper branch of one of the aspens by the road, as though it had once been a balloon, and then burst, and then dropped.

"How do you know there'll be a view?" I said to my father.

He laughed. Like I was a stupid kid to have asked. Then he got angry. He smashed the bottle he was carrying down.

"Why don't you just be happy," he said. "This is a hill." It was a very slight hill. I was not out of breath. "A hill means a view. A view means good business."

He turned and walked quickly down, in the direction of the truck. He did not call for us to join him, and for a moment I thought I might be stubborn and wait there in the woods till I was asked. But then I grabbed my brother's hand and we ran after.

My father put me in the driver's seat and told me what pedal I should push. He and my brother shoved the truck back, and over the rut. I saw my father through the glass of the windshield. My brother was too small to see. It should have been me out there pushing and him at the wheel, because I was older. I think I was stronger.

On the main road, my father began to sing. It was a funny German song he liked. Not one of the ones that, later, would cause my aunt to hit him with a spoon. It was one about a lady with a bun stand on the highway.

When we got near home, houses began to appear on the sides of the road. A white shape floated in front of us for half of an instant and then there was a bump and a smash.

"Fuck me," my father said, "what was that." I started to cry, and then my brother did too. "Be quiet, you kids," my father said, "we hit something."

He got out of the truck and went around to the back and got his gun from the rack. "Did you see him run?" he said.

"Which direction?" My brother and I shook our heads. We didn't see it run; it happened fast. "If it was a deer, we'll have some meat this season."

"It wasn't a deer, it was a dog," my brother said.

"How can you be sure?" my father asked. "You can't see from way back there."

He got the gun ready. "I'll put him out of misery, whatever it is. It's better that way."

We waited in the cab for half an hour. Then my father returned and dropped something heavy into the bed of the truck. He put his gun on the rack and got in beside me. "You were right," he told my brother, "it was a dog, but I got him. It's better that way. I hit him quite hard."

We drove the rest of the way home and no one said a word. My father's favourite country music station played. Then we got out and saw that a small dog's white head and part of his shoulders were stuck to the grille of the truck.

"This will be difficult to explain," my father said.

MY FATHER HAD TAKEN a can of orange spray paint and numbered the logs of the half-built hotel. "I'll build it exactly the same," he said, "on the hill."

My brother and I, on weekends, got paid fifty cents an hour to help my father in the yard. When we did not do much, he said, "I don't know if you earned this," but he always handed over exactly what we were due.

When all the logs had been disassembled and lay, in small piles, out in the yard, several years had gone by. I was almost in high school when the Caterpillar arrived. My mother said, "Make the most of it, Sasa, these are our final days. We're leaving you." But we stayed on all winter, and through most of the spring. My father went back and forth to the hill lot, and took his chainsaw with him. Each time he went he cut down a few trees and flattened the ground.

"Don't flatten it too much," my mother said, "or it won't be a hill anymore."

In late October he drove the Caterpillar into the coulee and it stuck. Then he went out each day with a shovel and stayed away until dark. He'd turn the Caterpillar engine on and leave the door open so that he could listen to the country music station while he shovelled and drank. Before the snow flew he put a blue tarp up and kept on working. In the dead of winter, still he went. The mud would have frozen even if the snow didn't get in through the tarp. We never went over to check what he did when that was the case.

The blue tarp was visible from the road, and every day we drove by it twice on the bus route, to and from school. In the spring—a few days before we left him—the tarp came down and my father drove the Caterpillar out of the coulee and parked it behind the house. He didn't mention the event, and neither did we. My mother began to park the station wagon on the side of the road, even though there was still enough room in the drive.

I WAS ALLOWED TO carry my own ticket, but my brother was not. I was not allowed to carry his. My sister, Emira, carried his, and she carried her own. In my own hand was my own ticket, and nothing more. When we stood on the platform, Emira said: We should guess the exact minute that the train will arrive. Emira was right. How did you do that, you must have cheated, I said. How would I cheat, she asked. Listen to yourself.

My mother gave us each a bun and a stick of cheese. If you eat it now, you'll be hungry later, she told us, but I ate mine right away. My brother saved his bun on his lap, and lay the stick of cheese beside it. All day, I watched the bun get dry and the cheese sweat. I told my brother, You should eat that now. Look, it's being ruined. Let me eat a little of it, I'm bigger than you and need more food. He said, No. I will wait a little longer. My mother slept in the seat in front of us. Her head was on the window. It bounced some-times but she did not wake up until it got light. How can she sleep, I asked Emira. *Hush*, Emira said. My brother, too, drifted off to sleep. His hand covered the bun in his lap and the cheese with its beads of sweat that had turned cold on top. I could not steal it. My father did not sleep. He walked up and down the car. Then, in the exact middle of the night, when everyone except us two, in the whole world, was sleeping, he turned in his seat and looked into my eyes. I did not intend this, he said. I nodded. But maybe it's better this way.

When my mother woke she gave us each another bun and another stick of cheese. Now my brother had two meals in his lap. Eat your food, said my mother, crossly. Don't act like a poor person. My brother said to me: You can have that bun now, and he stretched out his hand, with the stale bun in it, to me. I laughed in his face. I would not touch it.

ONE DAY, ON OUR WAY into town, we smelled a barbecue in someone's yard. I looked out the window and saw a low house, with the smoke of the grill rising up, over the top of the fence. The bent head of a man could be seen. He was wearing a hat.

"Do you ever wish," I asked my mother, "that we were a regular family, who did regular things?"

"Oh yes," my mother said, "all the time."

THE MORNING WE LEFT my father, he said he'd drive us in to school. He was like an animal, and sensed something in the air. We didn't tell him. "Let's go up to the lot after school," he said. "Let's clear a few trees, then go out for a meal." He talked the whole way to town, though in those days we almost always drove in silence.

"We'll cut hay this year," he said. "You kids will help. We'll get a horse. Be cowboys."

My mother picked us up after school with the boxes in the back of the station wagon, and then we unpacked them at an apartment in town. We didn't go back to my father's house for some weeks and when we did there was a note on the table that said, *I'm just out at the lot, I'll be back before long.*

"How did he know we were coming today?" my brother

said. I said: "How do you know that he wrote that this morning?"

AFTER THE WAR, my father's father came home, and for seven months he stayed. The neighbours wrote things on his wall, and on the stone outside his step. Worse than that. They did not like a German.

I'm not a German, my father's father said, but he took his children to Bavaria, and raised them near the border. His gentle wife he treated like a rag, but other than that he was a kind, and homesick, man.

NOW MY AUNT Emira says: "Ha! 'There wasn't a stick in the house,' the man says. It goes to show you the holes in his story."

Then my father starts to sing and Emira goes for the spoon. "I'm not saying Uncle Alen *wasn't* shot," he relents before she can hit him, "I'm just saying Nino was too. I saw him. Out on the lawn. Stretched, as though resting. We didn't have shoes."

"You fool," my aunt says. "You think they took the bed from under you? You think they took it while you slept?"

"I didn't sleep," my father says. "I haven't slept my whole long life." He starts to sing. Aunt Emira brings the spoon down—hard—on the table.

"Stop singing those songs," she tells him. "People will hate you. Your children will hate you. Do you want that? Do you want that, you dummy?"

"What's wrong with singing?" my father asks. Then looks up, and wags his head in a loop, as if searching for the cynic who might be hidden somewhere. "What's wrong with singing a song sometimes?"

"No one sings like that anymore," Emira says. "Or not that you'd remember. It's been years," she says, "since anyone who isn't crazy's sung a song like that."

She turns to my brother and then she turns to me. "I'm sorry for you," she says. My brother and I are sitting up, very tall and still, in our straight-backed chairs.

Our plates—recently—have been pushed away as far as we can push them.

"I'm sorry to tell you that your father is crazy."

My brother nods slowly.

"You're not even German," she informs my father, the spoon in the air. "You're Croatian," she says. "And now you live in the sticks of Red Deer, Alberta—face facts."

My father continues: "You were sleeping, and so you wouldn't have known. It was—exactly—the middle of the night. Everyone in the whole wide world, but me and our father, was sleeping. Only I and my father were awake in the world."

Aunt Emira hits my father again with the spoon so that his head bobs to the table and into his arms. He says: "He turned. He looked into my eyes. He put one hand to his heart. He said—" But his voice is too muffled by his sleeve.

"It's possible," my aunt says, "that the dog was simply making too much noise."

"He howled and would not stop," my father agrees.

Aunt Emira sighs. "I suppose it could have happened that the dog was also shot, but," she says, and shakes the spoon, "they did not take one stick of furniture from that house."

WHEN WE ARRIVED, months late, for the Christmas dinner, there was a note on the table. *I'm at the lot*, it said. *Make yourselves comfortable. I'll be back before long.*

But my father was not at the lot when we got there. He was stretched, instead, in his favourite living room chair. The television was on, but the sound was turned off.

"When did you leave us the note?" I asked him. "When were you up at the lot?"

My father turned the TV off. He smiled at my brother and me as we stood in the doorway.

Aunt Emira said: "A week ago. He hasn't been out of the house for a week."

"But," I said, and paused. "We didn't know ourselves we were coming, until the day before last," I said. "Who did you write the note to?"

My aunt waved the question away, but my father answered.

"I wrote just in case."

Emira nodded, and shrugged. Then shook her head at us, back and forth.

The artificial Christmas tree still stood in the corner, and my father got up then, from his chair, and plugged it in so that the coloured lights blinked on and flashed; on and off, on and off, in an irritating spiral.

BEFORE WE LEFT my father, we flew to Bavaria and rented a car at the airport and drove to the house of my uncle there. What my father recalls is the flight. How we were offered a seat in first class, and how for the first half of the trip my father sat up there, in front, and at the exact halfway point in the flight he got up abruptly and gave up the seat to my mother.

"They served me champagne," he said. "Called me sir."

Then he came to sit back in the regular section with my brother and me. He leaned over our two narrow seats to look out of the window, and pressed his knuckles up to the glass.

"When I was a boy, I thought I'd feel flying all over my body," he said. "Like when you dream it, I mean."

We drove around in the rented car and helped my uncle in the kitchen garden. I thought, If I'd been raised with a kitchen garden, things would have been different.

My grandfather was a happy man; he did not seem bad.

My mother disapproved of the way my grandmother wouldn't sit down with us at mealtimes to eat, and so she kept her company in the kitchen, and wrote recipes down in a yellow notebook, with blue cornflowers on the front, in a row. When, later, my mother made the meals at home and they did not taste the same as they had at my grandmother's place, she blamed the store-bought food and spices. "Things taste better that have been grown out-doors," she said. "That's why we moved to Alberta, to grow things outdoors. And now all we have in the yard is a Caterpillar and a taken-down house."

"Don't lose sight," she told me, "of the things in your life, in this way."

THE MEAL IS VENISON, and potatoes, and my aunt's fruit bread, which is so hard it needs to be wet down with water to eat. It's okay to say that the fruit bread is hard.

"That's the way it should be," my aunt Emira says. "It won't last if it's soft."

My father recovers himself somewhat and sits up again, and smiles, but doesn't speak until he's finished his beer. I think it's his last.

Then he says, "Tell your father what you need," and looks at my brother and me.

I say, "Don't worry about us."

Emira says, "You're happy, then?" She nods and nods her head, up and down. "Things are going well for you, in town?"

"Yes," I say. My brother nods, too. Just once: yes.

Aunt Emira clasps her hands at her chest and says, "Isn't that a blessing. Sasa, isn't that a blessing. You have two children—nothing to show for yourself, except that—and even when they come, three months late, for Christmas"— her voice rises in the way that it rises when she prays out loud in the yard—"and you've nothing to give them to take home to town—"

I didn't know that my aunt Emira got drunk, but now she is not making sense, and my father looks strange. I wish that I could stop things, and put them back. It is difficult to say now what will happen next, or if it should matter.

"Neither," my aunt continues, "do they—either of them—*need a thing in the world.* We should all be so lucky. Make mistakes like you, brother. Of such little consequence."

WHEN WE GET OUT of the train the light is beginning to fall, from the sky to the long shoulders of the track by the road. Everything looks bright and clean as if no one had touched anything. The track—stretching here one way, here another—cuts the hill in such a way that it appears to be the very limit of things.

After that there is only the sky, a dull and nearly absent blue.

My brother makes a small sound as though he is dreaming, but he is awake now; I believe he is happy.

In a little while, the light, too, will disappear, I tell my brother. And when it goes, then so too the track. Then so too the train and the grass (which is now just bare of snow, though not yet, I say, completely). But I and our father (I tell my brother so that he will not worry) will remain, unsleeping.

The sun, beginning to settle, startles itself on the grass, and jumps from dull blade to blade, and stays finally nowhere.

WHEN WE LEAVE MY father's house, my aunt gives each of us, my brother and me, a loaf of the heavy fruit bread to take home to my mother.

"She will have missed this stuff, too," my aunt says. "They make everything soft in the store."

My father is back in the den, with the TV's sound on now. "Say goodbye to him," we say to Aunt Emira. Then we scrunch our eyes shut when she hugs us, and go out to the car.

When we're in the car, I am very precise about putting it into gear. I spin the wheel in several firm rotations. I like to drive. I feel grown-up. I imagine my aunt and my father watching. Not saying anything to each other, but watching, each from a different vantage point of the windowed house, and thinking: It's true. Their lives have come together, in the way that they planned.

I do not think it's likely they're watching, but still I imagine that they are, and feel glad when we complete the turn in my father's drive without stalling the car, and begin to pick up speed, and pass the coulee, and head out to the highway.

I think: So this is how it feels to be a grown-up person. I look at my hands as if they belong to someone else. I feel neat, and gathered up within myself, as if I took a broom to the far corners of my body and swept myself clean into a pile.

CLARENCE

ALL MY LIFE, Clarence had lived at the top of the Lakehead road in a tall, upright house that looked just like my mother's. It wasn't, however, until I was eighteen years old—the summer I got a job working for the *Weekly Gleaner* in town—that I ever laid eyes on him.

Guy was the *Gleaner*'s editor-in-chief. He said Clarence was the oldest man in the county—probably even the state. It was hard to tell exactly, and even more difficult to prove. Clarence himself hardly knew anymore just how long he'd been alive. He didn't get around much, hadn't for a while. Not, at least, for eighteen years. Even the Save-Easy boy (who had grown, over the intervening period, into a surly, dough-faced Save-Easy man) never saw Clarence anymore when he went up to the house once a week, delivering the groceries and the mail.

But that was the summer of the fiftieth-anniversary spread, and Guy said he wanted Clarence right on the cover. I'd only just started, but he gave the job to me anyway. "Let the old fella tell you a thing or two," he said, when he sent me up the road. I could tell he thought that he was doing me a favour.

IT WAS CLARENCE'S WIFE, of course—twenty-five years younger—and not Clarence himself, who came to the door. She had taken her time, and when she did arrive, she opened the door only partway—hardly wide enough to pass. "Oh, it's you," she said. "Come from the paypah."

I nodded my head, and indicated my new camera, which I had purchased with my own money. She stared—first at it, and then at me—before, finally, opening the door a little wider. "Well," she said. "Come in. He sure ain't coming to greet you."

In the same way that people, over the years, come to resemble the things that surround them—their animals, their wives—Clarence had come to resemble his house. He was tall, even sitting upright in his living room chair. Straight as a chimney. And—like all the houses along the Lakehead road, where large families had long ago moved into town—mostly shut-up-looking, like only one or two rooms were lived in at all.

And old. Terminally so. His eyes sunk so deep in his head, like inset windows, that his skin, where his eyes should have been, ruffled out around them like curtains for the Fourth of July. His long neck was so thin and straight that his head seemed to be set there as if only temporarily. When, finally, I worked up the courage to speak, I did so quietly—afraid of disrupting what seemed to be a delicate balance. Even with how eager I was to get Clarence's name—and my own— onto the front page of the anniversary special, I didn't mind particularly when I saw that there was no story to find at

Clarence's house. Even when (cautiously) I managed to lift my voice, each of my carefully prepared questions was met only by a devastating silence. I was happy enough not to test the limits of that particular silence. Happy enough to take my leave as quickly and discreetly as possible, and—having gleaned nothing—simply head back to town. I had, in fact, just resolved to go when I discerned a low hum—a sort of sad, slow whistle, like a distant train—which (emanating, as it did, from Clarence's general direction) I took to be a form of reply. Still—and though I strained, desperately, to do so—I could not make out a single word. Once more, I resolved to make my departure.

But again I was checked by something. Again, I paused, cleared my throat, and read through the list of questions I had prepared earlier in the day. This time, though, the words stuck curiously in my throat; I nearly choked on them. I had not even reached the middle of the page when I stopped, mid-sentence. I wanted only to get away—and fast. What, I wondered, had possessed me to enter that house at all? To trespass that last, and most remote outpost at the end of the Lakehead road? What had I hoped to uncover there?

Still, for some reason, I remained. Setting my notebook and pen gingerly to one side, I sat, uncomfortably, as the low and wordless hum, which I had taken, just a moment ago, as a sort of reply, continued to echo—as though from a great distance—from the general direction of Clarence's large, and mostly emptied, frame.

Finally, I unpacked my camera and shot a roll of film as if at random. Then, and without announcing my intention to either Clarence or his wife—I let myself out the front door, and pretty well ran all the way back into town.

GUY WAS NOT so easily discouraged. Once he set his mind to something it was pretty well set, and that summer he was set on having Clarence on the cover of the anniversary special. "Don't worry," he said when I returned. "You'll try again tomorrow." He slapped me on the back, hard—in a way that he had no doubt hoped was encouraging—and was about to leave when he caught a glimpse of one of the photographs I had printed from my hastily shot roll, drying on the rack by the door. "Hey," he said, "that's not half bad." He pinched the print from its hold and looked at it more carefully. Then he handed it back, nodding gravely. "You could still make the covah," he told me—but now it sounded like a warning.

It was true; it was a fine picture. Clarence appeared just as he had in the dark living room earlier that day. His eyes nearly lost in his head, which sat perched above his wide, and by comparison large and unaltered, woodcutter's frame. In every photograph, and this one was no exception, his mouth appeared to be shut tight, a firm and single line.

"Now, see, it's all about the angle of the thing," Guy said the next day, as I prepared for my departure—taking longer than usual. He himself was leaned comfortably back in his bendable chair, which he would not be required to depart from—that day, or any other. I nodded. Though I could not imagine what possible "angle" might illuminate, with Clarence, any story at all—let alone one worthy of the anniversary special. Finally, there being very little to do in the way of preparation, and so no means of drawing it out any longer, I made my way to the door. "Tell me," Guy shouted after me—sensing my concern, which I had found difficult to hide—"tell me if there isn't a man alive won't say a few words for the front-page news."

Despairingly, I pulled the door shut behind me, muffling Guy's final words, but just as I did so—it hit me. I didn't know why I hadn't thought of it before. Like most good ideas, what had occurred to me then was very simple, so that now that I had thought of it, it seemed very obvious that I had. By the time I had arrived at Clarence's house, I was in a completely altered mood. Even the atmosphere of the old place seemed changed. Even Clarence (when, after once again being met at the door, I was led down the seemingly destinationless hall to join him) seemed different somehow. He seemed—more relaxed. Almost cheerful. Instead of the whispering ventriloquism of the day before, a heavy silence prevailed, but even this did not trouble me, so certain was I that my idea would in no time have us all—myself, Clarence, and Clarence's wife—smack on the front page of the anniversary special. It was true—it was all about the angle of the thing. At that very moment, Clarence's wife (who had once again greeted me at the door, saying, "I was starting to wondah if you was coming at all") was upstairs, readying herself for her own feature photo. Much to my relief, she had quickly agreed to the suggestion—disappearing hurriedly up the dark stairs, in order, she said, to change into something that would "suit." It was, of course, Clarence's wife—not Clarence himself—who could answer the few and simple questions I'd prepared, and fill in the gaps of the story. I simply had to wait.

And so, in the silence that did not weigh so heavily now, I began to tell Clarence a story of my own, about the time when I was fifteen years old and I saw a snake devour a trout, in shallow water, at the bottom of the Lakehead road. I don't know why that was the story I thought of just then. At first, I thought I might inspire Clarence to tell some story of his own. That an errant word might stir in him some long-forgotten remembrance—but after a while I forgot about Clarence almost altogether.

I had been out with my brother, Frankie—I said—in our uncle Trevor's boat. Uncle Trevor used to be married to Aunt June, but now he lived in Bangor, and didn't have a boat, and I never saw him. Frankie worked at the mill in town, but I hardly saw him either. Even when I did, it was like we hardly knew each other the way we always had to try so hard just to find something to say. But back then, it was different. We often went off together, sometimes for whole afternoons, and when we could find it to take—a couple of beers, or when we were especially lucky, some of Uncle Trevor's homegrown weed—we did, and drank it, or smoked it, or both, and felt for an hour and a half better than we ever had, or ever likely would again. It was as if it was not then—sitting at the edge of the lake in Uncle Trevor's boat, with a long line dropped straight down, which we never bothered to recast—but at every other time that the world was only half-real, and we were half-men, and full of illusions.

On that particular day Frankie had found a quarter bottle of Uncle Trevor's whiskey in the bottom of the boat, all wrapped up in a life preserver. When he found it, he gave a whoop and a holler, swinging it above his head for me to see, and then the two of us drank it down, all of it. Or what was left. Our eyes bugging out of our heads with all the effort it took not making a face. Then we sat around in the hot sun for some time. Not feeling real at all—or grown-up, or anything. After a while, Frankie staggered up and puked into the lake. I watched him, but it was hard. The whole world, and he with it, seemed to spin unsteadily in slow circles. I had to hold on to my head in order to make sure that it was not my head that spun. But no—my head stayed in its place, and the world spun. Something must have come unfixed inside me. Either that or the world—and my position within it—was a lot less solid than I had so far supposed. Perhaps this—I thought suddenly—was what dying would be like someday, when it happened. A beginning to . . . unravel somehow, break away. Until, finally, all the small and disconnected pieces that had somehow, inside you, mysteriously, and for so long, conjoined, began to slowly disentangle themselves from one another, be sent—spinning—away . . .

I did not, at first, hear Frankie yell. Or, rather, I heard the yell, but I did not hear Frankie. That was how disconnected everything had become. But finally I realized that it was Frankie who yelled. That the yell stemmed from a probable cause—was directed toward an equally probable effect. I got up reeling, dragging myself down in the direction of the lake. Then, there it was. The snake, his jaw slackened and unhinged, inching his way over the body of a fish, over three times his size, which had been floating, dead, in the shallow water.

It must have been nearly three-quarters of an hour before the snake finally swam away, the fish devoured. All that time, Frankie and I—even in the state we were in, or more likely because of it—watched. Both of us transfixed, unmoving. It was the only time I ever saw my brother approach anything close to what you might call *awe*. When it was over, and the snake—his belly stretched and fish-shaped—had swum unevenly away, Frankie said, "Wow! That . . . was *amazing*," and then he began to laugh in a way that I hadn't heard him laugh in a long time, even then, and I felt really sad for a minute when I heard him, because it made me remember that things had changed, and that being real and grown-up-feeling sometimes meant that also you didn't feel the way you used to feel. And that things were, from now on, going to keep on going that way;

and that has certainly turned out to be true. That afternoon, though, it was just Frankie, with his eyes all wide, looking at me, giggling in this funny way, and saying: "That was like a baby being born . . . *but different.*" So that then I started to giggle, too—managing only to say, "Yeah, but—*really*—*fucking*—*different,*" between fits, and then we nearly killed ourselves, doubled over, laughing, and finally I threw up.

I HAD BEEN INTENDING to tell Clarence just a bit of the story. Just the part about the snake, leaving out everything else. Get him going, I thought. Some line of his own. But then, when he didn't respond—when he only continued to stare, disinterestedly ahead, a slight smile on his face, as though he already knew everything and was only patiently hearing me out—I really did, I began to forget all about him. I began to flesh out the details; that was how Uncle Trevor's whiskey got in. And then the strange way I felt then. In the approximately three-quarters of an hour in which Frankie and I sat on the edge of the lake in Uncle Trevor's boat, watching a snake eat a fish. The way that, when I found my attention slip, in its reeling state—even for a fraction of a moment—away, I would say to myself, in that voice that spoke—that was still itself inside my brain—"This . . . is *extraordinary* . . ." and that would serve somehow, at once, to bring me back. I didn't know what for. Or why that word in particular was the one that came to mind. It was just the one that did, and I told Clarence about it. And then about how I had been thinking—just then, as I spoke, as Clarence and I sat, waiting together, for his wife to come downstairs finally, and finish the story—that maybe that's all you ever needed, really. To find, and hold on to, some extraordinary thing.

It wasn't until I had finished that I realized that Clarence was dead. That he had in fact been dead a long time. Perhaps all afternoon. I'm not sure now why it suddenly dawned on me then, instead of before—or, for that matter, why I had noticed it at all, and not continued to go on believing that he was alive. I just—all of a sudden—*knew*. It did not even surprise me. I got up slowly, and walked carefully from the room, plunging into the dark hall.

"Hello?" I called out, standing now at the bottom of the staircase, beyond which, some time before, Clarence's wife had disappeared. There was no response. "Ma'am," I called again. "Hello?"

Finally, she arrived. Down the long front stairs. In a costume dress with starched high sleeves, her hair done up in a stiff cascade, and at her throat a single strand of pearls. The pearls had been polished so bright that—even in the thin stream of light that, from a small slit in the blind of a hall window, had fallen on the stair (that light the one sign in the whole house that there existed an outside world at all)—they positively glowed.

For a moment she looked . . . divine. As though she were arriving not just from another region of the large house but from a distant planet.

"Well," she said, as she descended. "I never got a chance to wear it out. I'll get it in the picture, then at least it'll be used."

"Ma'am," I said.

"My sister sent it," she continued—the stairs nearly fully descended now. "From Farmington, some years ago. Not long after I was married. Still fits. Imagine!"

"Ma'am," I said again. "He's—" And paused a second time—unsure, suddenly, of how I should refer to the old man—what proper name to use, if any. "He's—dead."

IT WAS SHE, THEN, and not I, who led the way. Who entered the room, and crossed it with a steady tread. Who bent stiffly toward her husband in his chair—obscuring him with her puffed sleeves almost entirely.

Sure enough, Clarence was dead. I remained where I was—hovering at the door—while Clarence's wife rose and remarked that, indeed, what I had said was true. She smoothed the creases in the lapel of his coat, and centred the cap on his head. She didn't need to shut his eyes, because—tucked in their folds, like windows decked out for the Fourth of July—they were already quite as good as closed.

"He looks all right," Clarence's wife said then. Stepping back to get a better look. "He looks," she said, "the same as ever." Then, turning suddenly toward me, she said, "Well, that's some comfort anyway, isn't it? If death don't change a man," she said, "then, I guess—well—nothing woulda."

But she did not laugh. As I had expected that she might.

Perhaps it hadn't been a joke at all. That was what I wanted then. For it all to turn out to be a little joke. For her to laugh; to, with that laugh, convince me of something that I did not feel. And though there was no doubt that it would have been odd if she'd complied—if she had, at that moment, as I wished that she would, let out an uproarious shout—it would not have been so odd as what she did do.

Tugging once more at the starched collar of Clarence's shirt and spinning to face me—a hand resting now on a shoulder, on Clarence's large, almost unaltered woodcutter's frame—she said, "Well, where do ye want me?"

I did not understand, and only stared at her, blankly. "What?" I said. There was a new expression on her face now. An impatience. "For the pikcha," she said. Almost beseechingly. "I had," she explained—indicating the dress—"an awful job gettin' in."

So, because I could think of nothing else to do, I took her picture. Just in the way that she'd arranged it—which was, after all, quite the same as I'd imagined. A gloved hand resting on one of Clarence's high shoulders—in death still as straight and tall as Clarence's house, or any of the houses on the Lakehead road. His wife beside him—leaning ever so slightly forward, as if to meet the very limit of the frame. And smiling. Like a country pageant queen.

SIGNAC'S BOATS

For John

WHEN MARTHA FIRST met Charlie, and fell in love, she was still working at a place called Fat Albert's on the rue des Halles. It was an American place, but even the Americans pronounced the "Albert" as if it were French. Albert himself, who, to his face, everyone just called Al, was from Jacksonville, Florida, and had come to Paris at the age of twenty-two after reading *Giovanni's Room*. He made the best food that Martha had ever, or would ever, taste, although later she could never be sure if it was just that she never ate that much butter again. Chicken that fell from the bone. Five different kinds of potatoes. Okra that arrived from somewhere.

At night, the place was bursting. No one ever wanted to go home once they came, so they stayed, and ordered more bottles of wine until they were dancing. Shuffling out between tables. Knocking into those who—elbows out—were still eating, and using their hands. Sometimes it was hard to tell who was dancing and who was calling out for more hoppin' John or wings.

When Ginny introduced herself to Martha she said, "It's not so bad, if you don't mind feeling like a piece of meat yourself," but she loved it there, at Al's. Ginny was one of a dozen or so of the girls, all of them slim, and American, and pretty—just thrilled to pieces, like Martha was, to be in Paris, and not back home like everyone else. There were the great Nordic ice queens of the Midwest, the brunettes of New England, and two brash redheads: one from Washington State, and the other from somewhere in the Carolinas. Martha was from Port Jarvis, New York, near the Pennsylvania border, and rather old-fashioned looking—her hair a russet colour, something in between. Still—she was pretty, and could pass.

It was a sort of a joke that they all had French names. Martha was Chantelle, and Ginny was Lucille. They wore their names on the collars of their shirts, and with the growing roar of the restaurant crowd they would hear their names begin to echo from every corner of the room. "Chan-teeeelle," the customers would call out, in their American accents, affected or real. Sometimes other, less decorous names were called. It was the Americans who were the worst. They looked like outmoded GIs, as if thirty years hadn't passed, and they still came to Al's place when they got homesick, bored of the French girls in Pigalle. The worst she ever got, though, was a slap on the ass. Other than that, no one ever laid a finger on her, and the tips were great.

AFTER THEIR LATE SHIFTS, Ginny and Martha would find some quiet place where they could split a bottle of wine and count out their cash. Martha thumbed briskly through the bills, exclaiming the total in a single, jubilant note, but Ginny was more careful and divided hers into three neat and separate rows, writing the totals of each pile in the small black ledger book that she carried with her everywhere.

Ginny was going to be a Guggenheim. The first of the piles was for that. It was untouchable: gallery money. The second and larger pile was for art. Every month she allowed herself the purchase of a single piece, and so frequented the boutiques, when she wasn't working, in the affordable part of town. The third and smallest amount went, regretfully, toward the week's expenses—these, though, were next to nothing in those days.

All of Martha's own savings went toward getting herself "on her feet"; she had only just arrived and was still renting a room at Madame Bernard's. But then, nearly all at once after she met Ginny, she met Charlie, and then she didn't care particularly about "her feet" anymore. She didn't tell Ginny this, but Ginny knew. At their post-shift communions, when they drank too much wine, Ginny would say, regarding her own neat piles, "Really, Martha, it's just *so good* to have a *plan*."

But Martha, at that time, knew of only two kinds of plans, and one was for those, like her friends back at home, who had made them too simple and so were already done, and the other was for people like Ginny, who never would be. There didn't seem to be any plan for the kinds of things that Martha desired.

At the time, the closest she could come was Charlie.

the most surprising thing for Martha in those first months in Paris was that, although she had travelled all the way from Newark—that is, all the way from one side of the world to the other—she had not actually *seen* it. Not, anyway, in the way that they spoke of it back home—as if "the world" was a single, observable thing.

It was a disappointment to have to realize that her own limited perspective had neither increased nor lessened in France, but had remained, instead, stubbornly, the same. The street disappeared against the limit of the horizon at a vanishing point no farther away than it had in Newark—or even in Port Jarvis. The sounds of the pedestrians and traffic were no clearer or more relevant to the ear.

Overall, though, she was not dissatisfied, and it was this, perhaps, that was most bewildering. To realize that she had found—after all, and so simply—everything that she might need or desire not only in a place that, like Port Jarvis, was single and measurable, but in a *person*, in Charlie—a person who (she was beginning to suspect), much as she loved him, would turn out that way, too.

It seemed that there would, after all, be much of the world that Martha would just let go—unnoticed and undesired.

Once, Martha made the mistake of mentioning something along these lines to Ginny, and Ginny, in her "learn from me" tone, had said, "You're *always* going to be capable of wanting *more*, Martha." It had been one of their after-Albear specials. "The trick," Ginny had said, "is being satisfied with what you've got."

Ginny herself seemed satisfied just for saying it.

"Funny for you to say" is what Martha said. Her feelings were hurt even if she otherwise would have agreed. "I've *been* being satisfied. You're the one who wants to be a Guggenheim."

Ginny snorted through her nose. "It's not like *that*," she told Martha. "It's not about being some*one*, some*thing*. It's about—" she paused and looked at Martha, shaking her head, "having something to work *toward*," she said. "It's about *Art*."

Martha snorted, too. "It's about *nothing* is what it's about," she said. And then, made brazen by argument and wine, she continued, pointedly: "And I don't like your art."

Ginny was not offended. She rolled her eyes. "You like *pictures*, Martha," she said, and then, as if she were addressing an invisible audience beside them: "Let's get one thing clear before this discussion goes any further. Martha doesn't like *art*, she likes '*pictures*.'"

Martha liked Charlie's art though, and Ginny knew it. And it wasn't just because she liked Charlie. Even some of the more abstract things that he did, like a purplish splash, or a study of a red ball that looked like a badly drawn version of the Japanese flag. He'd given that one to Ginny, and Martha had even been a bit sore about it at the time. To Martha he had always given the simple landscapes, and one time a sketch of a girl who didn't even really look like her.

"I just think there has to be—some kind of story," Martha said. Although more tentatively now.

"*Martha*," Ginny said, again in her "learn from me" tone, "don't you see that's *so limiting?*"

"At least," Martha said irritably, "it's real. Limitations," she said, "are real." She was beginning to get upset but didn't know why. Any other time she would have just let it go.

IN TRUTH, MARTHA DID NOT know if she believed what she said, and she certainly did not only like "pictures." She found this out one day while still living on the Left Bank with blind old Madame Bernard, when Madame had introduced her to the bookcase of Monsieur Bernard, her dead husband—a professor at the university. She and Madame had leafed together through the heavy pages of Signacs and Seurats, and then they came to a book that Monsieur himself had written. Madame traced her hand over the cover to find her husband's name embossed there in raised letters, then she took Martha's hand and made her feel it, too, even though she could see it quite plainly. The book had large, smooth pages, as though blank, but Madame passed her hand over them anyway, just as she did her books in Braille.

When later Martha, on her own, examined the books more carefully, she found that they were scattered with cross-references and addenda: all of Monsieur's old yellowed notes taped into the margins, which defined and explicated each technique and style. In one of the books' opening pages there was an underlined quotation beside the word *Chromoluminarisme*, for example, which Martha roughly translated as "Make of art an exact science!!!"

So it was from Monsieur Bernard's bookshelves—from the forgotten, mostly unreadable notes of a dead professor, obscure even to his wife—that, on the quiet days at the beginning of her stay in Paris, Martha discovered the law of simultaneous contrasts and found, to her surprise, that she was not a lover of pictures, or of stories, as she had always supposed, but—like Monsieur Bernard—a *scientist* at heart.

Though the images were often blurred badly in the old books, Martha pored over the small isolate points of the later Signacs, attempting to see them at first as just that: singular, and insignificant. She found that then, when she stood back to look at the complete image, it was as though for a moment both things existed: the smallnesses and the whole, though no single mark in the images ever touched another, or blended in colour or tone. This sort of exercise could be frustrating with the badly copied old books, but when Martha landed the job at Al-bears, she took herself often to the Jeu de Paume, where she spent hours in front of the Signacs, especially the boats.

Again and again she marvelled over the manner in which the small points of colour maintained themselves independently of the image they conveyed, while at the same time they *gave themselves up to it entirely*. Like a mosaic, she thought, except the reverse, because instead of being scattered and then brought, suddenly, to a whole, it was apparent that with the paintings (which had no natural compulsion toward smallness or disjunction) it had been the painter who deliberately chose the fragmentation every time.

What the point was, exactly, of such division, if the image would after all turn out to be a large and straightforward thing, was something that troubled Martha. But always, over top of any doubts, there was that other thing: a confusion, a nearly religious sensation of wonder or awe. She found that, in looking at the paintings in their full, imposing, and somewhat muted form (the dots, she realized, were of course so much more spread apart than they had appeared on the shrunken page, and it was both a disappointment and a joy to her to find out that in fact the *holes did show*), this larger, stranger feeling always overshot the worry, so that she went away always palpably impressed.

MARTHA NEVER TOLD GINNY about Monsieur Bernard, or the boats, and fell into the defence of "pictures" mostly because she despised Ginny's snobbery. She continued to defend them even as she began to realize that what she admired in Signac was not the pictures themselves but their reverse: the practical assembly of the image on the page. She argued, privately to herself, that it was different with Signac. That with him there was always still the *picture*, the image, the *life conveyed*. Still the picnic in the park, and the tall parasols. Still the boats at the river.

It was Seurat who disturbed her. The way that with his bold lines and colour he could profess to direct his paintings through his stroke and tone alone; his dark and descending lines confidently occasioning sadness, for example—warm and cool tones, in equal measure, occasioning calm.

The bright ascending lines, of course, were joy.

Martha did not like to feel (when she stood in front of the paintings and felt just the way that Seurat and his lines had predicted) that it all had to do purely with optics and geometry. Though at heart she was a scientist, she certainly did not want things to turn out to be as simple as that.

So maybe she was not a scientist after all; it depressed her that her ideas and reactions could be so tediously accounted for. But when, one day, she admitted all of this to Charlie, he was not even surprised. She was still working at Al-bears then, and they were sitting out back, on crates that had been propped up sideways for them to smoke on. Exactly one month later Al would be beaten to death outside the La Chapelle Métro, and the restaurant would suddenly close.

"I don't see why you think they're so separate," Charlie had said. "Science" (he weighed it, heavily, on the one hand) "and art. It's only lately—it's only—*human beings*" (and he said the words as if they meant something different from what the words themselves supposed) "who've come up with the ridiculous idea to set them at odds."

He looked at her then, and leaned in, so that his shoulder pressed against her own. It was true that they had often been happy together.

For example, already Martha was not thinking of what

she had been saying, but was instead imagining herself as
. . . a field mouse, or some other creature—precognitive.
Who had not yet been, and never would be, set so at odds . . .

She found the image hard, but still there was something
in it a little like the feeling she got standing in front of Signac and his boats. Maybe it was not really altogether different, that feeling. From the one that the field mouse had. Of
everything collided, and occurring at once, and for a very
brief moment she existed like that, next to Charlie: a simple form. Looking out at the world as though from almost
underground—everything from that position appearing
blurred, and without distinction.

It was not only her imagination. She was, indeed, a small
and a simple creature in those days, when she first knew
Charlie. When, for what seemed like the first time, things
were happening to her like in other people's lives, and the
little distinctions that she'd made for herself, prior to that
time, had begun, slowly, to fade away.

This, she realized, of course, was love. It was the first
time she'd known anything about it and felt surprised that
it had in fact *simplified* her, when she'd thought it would
have made her at the same time more integral, and more
complex. As if she would have suddenly found herself a
functional thing, like a clock, or a television, with an infin-
ite number of separate mechanisms and parts that worked
on their own, and she knew what for, and why.

Cleats

For Peggy

THE CLEATS HAD BEEN received from Carey himself on the occasion of her fifty-second birthday. Fay had opened them up after the meal and, to the amusement of their guests, tried them on in the middle of the living room—making small dents in the carpeting. They looked like any ordinary pair of tennis shoes: blue canvas, with three white stripes. But on the bottom, where a soft rubber sole would otherwise have been, was a hard plastic plate studded with blunt nubs. Everyone exclaimed that they had never seen anything quite like them. "Carey! He's always had such a sense of humour." "Who would have thought? *Garden* cleats! Well, quite practical, really!" "Or nearly so . . ."

Carey had grinned at her from across the room, making his exaggerated eyes at her: a demonstration of the true sentiment that they both still assumed—even after all those years—he really did feel and would have expressed to her then, if it had been within his capacity to do so.

It turned out that the cleats were indeed only "nearly" practical, because it was only a few days after that that Fay got stuck in the yard. She'd wandered out, leaving her shoes on the flagged stones of the patio, and at first had paced easily, back and forth, along the sloped edge of the lawn. But then, descending to where the grass dipped suddenly and a drain drew the water to the gutter of the drive, Fay felt the cleats stick more firmly in the wet dirt; there was a little popping sound as they stuck. She shifted her weight from side to side in an effort to free herself, but that only seemed to work her in more deeply.

At first, it was not panic. It was only a dull, half-remembered flavour of something, a taste that she couldn't name, and didn't wish to. She continued to stand, her arms outstretched as though afraid she would fall, though she was not off-balance—then, tentatively at first, as if she was joking, she called out. For Carey, who she knew was somewhere in the house. When he didn't come, she called louder. Then again, louder—leaving less and less time in between calls for him to actually arrive.

It was Eva who came. Nonchalantly, to the upstairs window. Her bedroom overlooked the small lawn. "What's *wrong?*" she asked, letting the syllables drag. From her perspective, there was nothing at all *wrong* with her mother. She was only standing, as she'd often done, in the middle of the lawn. When Fay explained about the cleats—a little sheepish now, ashamed of herself for shrieking, and wishing it had not been her daughter to discover her—Eva laughed so hard that her head disappeared below the window. "Mom!" she said, when she returned, through bursts of laughter. "Just take the damn things off!" So Fay bent down, as her daughter had instructed, and took off the cleats. She stepped in her sock feet onto the grass. Without the cleats it was just the moist lawn underfoot and, sturdily on the ground, she reached down and tugged them from the wet dirt. They came up easily. She could still hear Eva from the upstairs window. "Are *you okay?*" Eva was saying, in false concern. Still laughing. "*Mom,* are you *all right?*"

IT WAS EVA, THOUGH, that Fay paused over, and not Carey, when three months later, in early September, she left them both and moved to Paris to live with Martha. Eva herself seemed hardly to notice the event. She had just entered her second year at a private college not far from their home, and seemed only very minimally aware that she had parents at all. Carey, on the other hand, called every day—sometimes two or three times in an hour—and left messages on her portable telephone until the message box filled. He wondered where Fay "got off," that's how he put it, assuming she'd some different set of rules to live by than everyone else in the world. She had, Carey said, over and over again, "chosen a life"—and now, he said, a touch of hurt in his voice, like a child, that life *needed attending.* It caused in Fay, briefly, in the moment that she heard it—that *thing* quivering there in his voice, canned in the telephone, on the other end of the line—a sweeping sadness, the depth of which she was not brave enough even to properly feel, let alone gauge or understand.

But then, when she repeated Carey's words to herself in her own head, what he had *actually* said, she could not help picturing the life that Carey described as the small and somewhat neglected houseplant that she'd left on the kitchen windowsill, which she did not care for.

Eva, though. At the thought of her, Fay would feel sorry for everything all over again. It really was such a shame, the way you could be so careful, and for so long, and then go ahead and undo it all in the end, as though nothing had ever been held together by anything at all.

EVA HAD ALWAYS had what Fay and Carey referred to as an "overactive mind." What other child (Fay would ask herself sometimes with no small degree of pride) might arrive home from the fourth grade with a new government system worked out on a scrap of paper—claiming that she'd figured out a way to "make everybody really happy." It turned out that what Eva had come up with was, essentially, Communism, but Fay had applauded the effort anyway. She'd added, however, and in no uncertain terms, that one or two other people had come up with Eva's idea before—and what the outcomes had been. "The ideas are good, though," she'd told Eva. "You keep having ideas." And Eva had. But each time there was some new flaw that, necessarily, Fay would feel obliged to point out. In order, she said to both Carey and herself, that Eva would not later be unduly surprised or disappointed by the world—and the way that ideas did or did not work upon it.

But then one day Eva could not get out of bed, and Fay realized that she had made a serious mistake. In truth, they had thought at first that it was only a resurgence of the

mild case of Lyme disease Eva had experienced the summer before, but shortly afterward it became clear that nothing in fact was—physically, at least—wrong with Eva at all.
When they admitted it, and went to see the psychoanalyst
instead, Fay felt ashamed. Like everyone else of her generation, she'd extolled the virtues of therapy for years, but had
always imagined (as it now became clear) that it applied to
other people—whose lives had not been, as Eva's had, so
carefully considered, and arranged. Her own troubles, or
those of her friends—their respective faltering careers and
marriages—she easily understood. There were always the
usual (outside, and unaccountable) factors to be considered.
Inattentive fathers. Catholicism. A generation of mothers
who thought that pain medication and jelly doughnuts
were good antidotes to an adolescent in the house. As silly
as it now seemed, it appeared that Fay *had truly believed* that
unhappiness in its different forms existed in the world only
through a series of avoidable blunders. In the summer of
Eva's paralysis, however, Fay was forced to admit that these
were blunders that she too had somehow, inadvertently,
made. Carey tried his best to comfort her: "You're not the
only thing in her life, you know," he said. "She's a smart
kid. She's too smart. She notices things."

Eva did, it turned out, have a certain rare disease. It was
some comfort to Fay, just to have it be *called* something. In
what Carey (insulted) referred to as his "layman's terms,"
the doctor described the manner in which their daughter had only *tricked* her body into feeling a pain that did

not, in fact, exist at all. Eva's mind, the doctor told them, had essentially sent out *alarm signals* to her body (pain, he had added, in brackets, for Carey and Fay) in preparation for a trauma that never actually arrived. Now both mind and body needed to be persuaded that the pain was superfluous. That the trauma was a figment of her imagination. Almost a narrative device, which her mind had employed in lieu of any other adequate means.

All of this was at first perhaps even harder for Carey than for Fay to grasp. He was a methodical man with a quick mind, and was therefore used to understanding things right away. He was in fact so used to this that he no longer believed in anything that he didn't immediately comprehend. At first, therefore, he didn't believe in Eva's disease either. He had scoffed at the doctor and his "layman's terms," which had succeeded only in convincing him that the doctor himself didn't have a clue what he was talking about. It seemed unthinkable to Carey that if his daughter was experiencing pain, it was not a legitimate effect stemming from a legitimate cause. "How could that possibly be a real disease?" he asked Fay. "Pain is pain," he said. They had been assured, however, that although the disease was rare, it was not abnormal, whatever that was supposed to mean, and although Carey was, eventually, somewhat appeased by all the explanations (lay or otherwise) of the medical validity of his daughter's affliction, Fay became only more convinced by all of the reiteration that the *real cause* of her daughter's illness was neither physical nor psychological, but stemmed instead from a sudden and extreme loss of faith, which she herself was directly responsible for.

Eva was hospitalized for the rest of that summer, and, until she forced herself to walk again, was refused everything that was substantial enough to be taken away. Parents' visits. TV. Books. Any somewhat edible food. These were returned slowly, as she began to progress. At first, they were disappointed in her advancement—her weight and her spirits continued steadily to diminish. Her legs, already thin, had begun to look useless and frail. Fay had panicked again—terrified that there had once more been some mistake, and that Eva's affliction was purely physical after all. She couldn't tell anymore what she wanted to be true. The doctor reassured her. It was certainly a "stubborn" case, he admitted, but there was no cause to worry. Eva would be walking again—he added encouragingly—very soon. And it was true.

That was at the beginning of September. By October Eva was back at school, easily making up the schoolwork she had missed, and seeming curiously optimistic.

FAY DID NOT RECOVER quite so rapidly, and continued to blame herself for her daughter's ordeal—citing, to Carey, different and often conflicting logic in order to prove her own guilt. It must have been, she would tell him, in those early years, before she *knew any better*. "That's what everyone is saying now. Did you know that?" she'd ask.

"That the damage done to a child in those foremost years makes almost every effort afterward practically obsolete? It must have been then," she'd say. Carey, however, even when pressed, could not remember this careless period at all, and truth be told, neither could Fay. When she first mentioned it to him, he had said only: "That's ridiculous. You've always been terrific with Evaline. I don't know what you're talking about."

But men, Fay thought, were very often oblivious to these, and other, things.

Almost overnight, however, after the illness, Eva grew up. Not entirely (there were strangenesses, things that worried Fay still), but, for the most part, Eva became, in teenagehood, a *teenager*. No one could have been happier than Fay when Eva stormed through the house in a violent temper, or suddenly began talking on the phone at all hours to God-knows-who. *This*, Fay told herself, was normal. This was the manageable stuff. The old irregularities lingered, of course—but they manifested themselves in small ways, now. She had a terrific fear of insects, for example. She wouldn't scream or run, like Fay would sometimes, but would instead grow very pale and still until someone noticed and steered her from the room. Then there were the "fad" fears, which were as irritating as they were troubling. One week, for example, Eva would be so afraid of dying in a road accident that she would refuse to ride in the car—but then the next week, and with no seeming transition, the car would be forgotten, and it was elevators that she steered away from. Then it would be the curb of the road, and several months would go by in which she left a wide berth between herself and the street, making crossing at intersections difficult. Still, though, as time passed and *teenage*hood more and more took its hold, these things diminished as well, until it seemed that Eva was an ordinary person with only very abstract fears of things.

She remained, of course, an intelligent child, with what her parents continued to refer to as an "overactive mind," and so she was never unaware of the eccentricity of her behaviour. Sometimes Fay would wonder what she was paying the therapists for, when it was Eva who seemed to be able to articulate everything—the trajectory of her fears, their probable root causes, and incongruencies—so much better than any adult with whom these issues had so far been discussed. The insects, for example. Eva would puzzle over it out loud sometimes, like it was a riddle—or somebody else's problem. She calculated, for example, the likelihood of dying from an insect bite in North America, and it was something so ridiculously small that she admitted without qualm that the possibility was more or less absurd. "We must just fool ourselves into thinking we're rational," she said once, after a similar exercise, "as a mechanism for survival. I mean," she explained to Fay, "if we *think* we're rational, but clearly are not, we can justify anything."

Fay and Carey had somewhat relaxed once Eva was safely in college. She seemed to adjust well and, to Fay's surprise, even joined one of the sororities and involved herself in their affairs. Fay had always been against that sort of thing, and she was (she even admitted this to Carey) somewhat disappointed that her daughter would need to resort to such "institutional forms of acceptance." Carey replied that—probably—institutional forms of acceptance were "just exactly what she did need," and Fay tried to content herself with that.

FAY FEARED THAT her departure—certainly a large-scale disruption from the regular order of things, which she had always attempted to maintain—might upset what she had always assumed to be, for Eva, a fragile balance, but, to the contrary, the departure seemed hardly to register at all. It was difficult to tell, though, because Eva refused to discuss the situation. On Fay's less optimistic days, of which there were many, she surmised that this refusal on Eva's part indicated that the damage was, indeed, running deep. This did not stop her from remarking, however (harshly, in a moment of frustration, which she later regretted), "Well, isn't irrationality a convenient *mechanism for survival*," which was something that had stuck with her, like many things that Eva said over the years. Eva—immovable—had only calmly told her mother that, according to her theory (which Fay, she said, had abused), it was Fay herself who was acting irrationally, and *Fay* who needed, desperately now, to "justify" things. "You know," Fay said, as calmly as she could, "you don't know as much as you think." She hadn't the least clue if this was true, but she had to say something.

It was frustrating, though—to have finally taken such an enormous step and have it go more or less unnoticed. All through that first fall Eva would continue to speak to her mother as though she had called up from the Redwood Plaza on the corner, instead of all the way from Paris, France. As though she had only stepped out for some "therapeutic overspending," as she often had before, and that she would undoubtedly return, just as from those earlier excursions (the possibility that she would not being so disproportionately small . . .), milder, a little abashed, and with an apparent sense of fresh commitment toward their—touchingly—ordinary lives.

Even Carey, after the initial shock, and those first few weeks, within which the messages piled, pretty well stopped calling. He was waiting for her, he said, to "come to her senses." This was just about what Fay had predicted. Carey, she'd told Martha after her first week in Paris, was, as the "ultimate human being"—a term she applied disparagingly—capable of adapting himself to anything, given enough time.

On the contrary, it took Fay three months to leave Carey after she had decided to do so, and then another three months to discover why she had. It wasn't, that is, until Eva was visiting over her Thanksgiving break in November that Fay at last connected the panic she had felt rising steadily within her, as she had stood in her garden cleats, stuck out in the yard, to the one other, half-remembered occasion in which she had felt that way before.

As always, it was just some silly thing—something that Eva had said, a particular note in her voice as she said it—that served to remind Fay of that original occasion. But when she did recall it, she recalled it in such perfect and immediate detail that it seemed to be no more distant a recollection, suddenly, than the memory of only six months prior.

Fay and Martha had still been in high school at the time—though just barely. They would graduate in June, and it was already spring. It was a Saturday, and as usual, the five of them—Martha, Fay, Laurel, Marilyn, and—oh, but that was right. Linda had not been with them that time. It had happened on the weekend that Linda was away—visiting Mount Holyoke and William and Mary. A boyfriend of Marilyn's (whose name and identity escaped everyone's notice even then) had taken Linda's usual place in Bobby Zerembeh's car. So, of course—there was Bobby Zerembeh himself. The wonderful Bobby Zerembeh, who married Laurel within a year and a half, but was Martha's—as everything seemed to have been Martha's—then.

Axel's was the only place they knew of that would let them drink without any trouble. It was in the next town over, and they could only get there on Saturdays when Bobby borrowed his father's old beat-up Rambler. When he did, they would all pile in—the five girls and Bobby—and drive the twenty minutes out on the back roads, because they preferred to take their time. It was, after all, those moments in the car before they arrived—when everything was about to, but nothing had happened yet, and the whole night spread ahead of them as if it belonged to someone else—that were the most precious. Once they arrived, and tumbled out, everything seemed to happen at once. They would be drunk almost right away just at the sight of the place—and then all over again on a pitcher of beer apiece, each for two dollars.

You could see New Jersey from Axel's, because of the way that the place was set out right there at the edge of nowhere. From that point—just outside of Axel's swinging door—there stretched only a large expanse of marshland. Then, on the other side of it, there were lights, and that was New Jersey.

Never once did they see another woman at Axel's, but the men didn't seem to mind it when the girls came. They were courteous and even gentlemanly—most of the time. The girls practised flirting, and bummed cigarettes. The men all slapped their thighs ironically by way of invitation, but they didn't kid themselves. Sometimes one of the girls, for a bit of a laugh, would sit down for just a fraction of a second on a proffered knee before she got up again, shrieking, to her feet—as though surprised to have encountered anything alive. The rest of them would be nearly doubled over in a corner, from laughing so hard. Bobby would be there too, of course, but with his eyes averted.

To Martha, and so to Fay, and to the rest, the men at Axel's were an *experience*—and experience they knew (of whatever kind) would stand them in good stead when someday confronted with the *real thing*. In return, the girls were gracious as could be; they didn't judge the men, or let them be judged, and even condescended sometimes to love them in an awful, sad sort of way. Even, or particularly, if there was something vaguely appalling about them. If they had no teeth, say, or gave one of the girls' bums a pinch as they were dancing. "Isn't it just—just so—*awful and sad?*" they would say to one another as Bobby drove them the long way home.

They were (even in those years, which later they thought of as their *cruel years*) capable of being tremendously *touched* by things. That was what Axel's was like. Like being *touched* to the quick by something outrageous, and bracing, and strange. When they felt that way, the whole place— that little rundown bar, right out at the edge of everything, from where you could see New Jersey—would suddenly feel warm and bright, and Fay would feel so full to the brim with something that she thought she might burst.

What it was she was filled with she didn't know then, and never would. She was only afterward able to recall the feeling through things that seemed to have so little to do with her, or with anything, that she wondered if she had really ever felt that way at all. It would come back, for instance, sometimes—just a hint of it—in the occasional black and white images she saw (not a *scene* so much as a flicker—as though *between* images) on a blanched TV screen. Or else it would be the clattering sound of silverware—the sound of other people's meals being eaten, with great pleasure, from a distance. Why either of these things would bring anything to mind for Fay at all—let alone the *full-to-bursting* feeling that she had got sometimes on the Saturday evenings of her youth—was a great mystery. Especially the silverware. No one ever ate anything but peanuts at Axel's place.

About halfway through the night, though, the feeling would change again. She wouldn't feel light anymore, like in the movies (the blanched light, the weightless clattering of silverware), but heavy and dull, instead—as though she'd absorbed a blunt object exactly the same size as herself. For whatever reason, Fay always appeared to the others in these moments almost *too* self-assured, and the girls avoided her—though not with contempt. Left alone, she would idle by the bar for a while looking unapproachable—until, without hardly knowing why, she would get up and run outside, swinging the door back and forth on its hinges behind her as she went.

She would run only a little ways, though, before she stopped, and though no doubt—at least in part—it was *fear* that stopped her, she never would have admitted to it. In her mind, Fay would have run all the way to New Jersey, if she'd wanted to. It was something else that stopped her. She didn't want, suddenly, to just *run away*. Just—anywhere. For two or three minutes, then, she would stand outside not wanting to run away, but not wanting to go back either. In those moments, it seemed impossible that anyone else was awake or alive in the world. Even the sounds from the bar seemed distant—as though they already had more to do with a memory of something. She tried to feel something. Some particular way. About the stretch of grass, for example. Or about herself. About the way she was then, or the way she was going to be. But she always got cold very quickly standing out there like that, and then, almost imperceptibly, bored, and she would start to wish that Martha—or better yet, Bobby—would come running out after her, and be concerned, and yell her name so that she would have no choice but to forget it all, and go back, and not have to feel any particular way about anything. When neither Martha nor Bobby did come, as they often did not, she'd wonder why, and feel hurt—and then jealous of Martha, who had *everything*—though *everything*, in those days, really meant only one thing: Bobby. It would never have occurred to either of them to be jealous of any of the other girls—and least of all, Laurel.

If no one came—as, again, they often did not—Fay would have to *make a scene*, like in the movies: she'd have to stumble in, knock into a chair, crash to the ground if she was able. In order that Bobby would have to get up from wherever he was and come over to her and ask if she was all right. Other times, she poked her head inside the door instead, and yelled, "Come on! Let's run across to New Jersey," and make as if she was really going to do it this time. Maybe she even believed that she really would do it, too, if no one came along to stop her.

But they always did, and that night it was no different. Then they piled into the car—all of them except for Linda—and began the long drive on the back roads home.

Perhaps it was just that: Linda being gone. But somehow that drive home was not like any of the other drives home. Something had shifted, and it even occurred to Fay that the great *change*, which they had all been anticipating with such eagerness but could never envision, or even properly believe in, had actually begun. Perhaps it was just that. The idea of Linda, back at school the next day, all aglow, talking about Mount Holyoke and William and Mary—choices that Fay and Martha scoffed at, preferring the state schools, where the men, at least, would be interesting, and you could actually *learn something*. Whatever it was, Fay found herself unhappily staring off down the long distance of the road, as if it were the distance to New Jersey. Wanting to be there. For real this time. Or in the empty field that stretched in between—which was neither here nor there, but instead nowhere in particular. To really *know* that field. To think it and think it, and never get cold, and never get bored. In short: she wanted to be anywhere but in that car, on that *interminable* road. Squished in the back with Marilyn, and that boyfriend of hers, whoever he was—irrelevant even then.

Up front was Martha, of course. She was sitting in the middle—between Bobby, who drove, and Laurel. Laurel, saying something in a sad, faraway voice, like in the movies, about Linda. Missing Linda. Saying: This is how *it happens*. How it begins. How *everything changes* . . . Fay, irritable in the back seat, saying: "Linda wouldn't have fit." Even though it struck her as interesting and a little disappointing that Laurel had been thinking the same thing that she had just a moment before. Interesting that Laurel had been thinking at all . . . But then what she said—about Linda not fitting—had made Laurel start to cry, and she sounded awful when she cried. The effect was not at all touching, like in the movies. When people cried in the movies it always seemed to do with everything all at once, and not just the thing that they were crying about. Martha would have been able to make it like that if she was the one crying. Fay, even, would have had a better shot at it. But Laurel was so plain, and so depressing when she cried, that it was as if the sad thing that she was crying about really was just that sad thing.

At first, Fay wished only that Laurel would shut up and not cry, but then she forgot about Laurel. She felt a growing pressure behind the ears. Then—a field rose before her. Stretched like a canvas. So that for the first time, she saw it. Truly. In panoramic vision—from all sides. There was no end to it this time—no New Jersey in the distance. It was just, for the first time, an uninterrupted vision of that which stretched, toward nowhere in particular, *in between* everything. But then, suddenly, it was not a vision at all. It *was* the field. Beamed into existence by the headlights of Bobby Zerembeh's car as he swung it from the road. And then it was Laurel. Scrambling like an animal at the door. And the scream. She felt it rather than heard it at first, but then she heard it, too. An inhuman sound. Then Bobby, who had turned around in his seat. Slapping her—quite hard—across the face, with the back of his hand. Finally, the scream stopped, and she realized it had been her own.

It had only been a small accident, and in under half an hour, the two boys—with the help of Fay herself, who had become remarkably calm by then, in that way that made the other girls leave her alone—had the car back on the road. With the exception of Martha, who had received a few bruises and scratches from Laurel as she had attempted to escape, no one had been hurt.

IT WAS MARTHA, and not Fay, who later spoke of the event if it was spoken of at all. Fay herself did not think of it; in fact, she did not even properly recall it, and over the years, because of this, she had come to think of the experience, to a certain extent, as Martha's own. Perhaps this was why it had taken six whole months to remember that it was *that particular moment*—the long extended moment leading up to the scream in which the scream had occurred—that she'd recalled and in some way experienced again, all those years later, when she wore the cleats that Carey had given her for her fifty-second birthday, and got stuck in her yard.

Like all of Martha's stories, this one had been told variously over the years. Sometimes, she spoke of it as a "falling-through time," a "flash," a "primal scream." When Eva visited, and the story of the scream again resurfaced, Martha said: "For your mother, it was like a sudden glimpse of—" and closed her eyes. How could she put it? What word fit now? At this juncture, after so much had changed? "Like a sudden glimpse . . ." Martha said again, finally, her hands floating in the air—not quite descending—"of the . . . the old-fashioned *horror of things.*"

Eva raised her eyebrows and looked hard at Fay, then Martha. "The—what?" she said. She was sitting opposite Fay, on Martha's couch, her feet tucked up under her. There was something surprising about the way that she sat. A certain—*composure* about her that Fay could not have anticipated. It made her want to cry, suddenly. It made her feel terribly—alone. But glad, too, in a way. Glad to be alone, if that was what it took. For her daughter to be sitting there, as she was just then—opposite her in Martha's living room—looking, for all the world, as if she had grown up by herself, without context.

"Oh, of it all . . ." Martha was saying to Eva, in reply. "The *old-fashioned horror* . . . of *it all.* The, how would you put it," she said, "the unravelling . . . Linda gone, you know—" Martha looked at Fay, "and us too, at the *verge* of something . . ." Then she paused, and her voice changed. "And the . . . fickleness," she said, laughing, "of that bitch Laurel's love."

The story had in fact been told by Martha in response to something Eva had asked earlier in the evening, though by now the question had certainly been forgotten by Martha—and no doubt by Eva as well. "Does it get any easier?" Eva had asked, even rolling her eyes a little as she said it—

conscious, as ever, of the way that everything (particularly the petty miseries of a college sophomore) was predictable, inevitable; had already *been done.*

Fay, too, had thought of Axel's for some reason when Eva said it, and so it seemed natural to her that Martha should have mentioned it then. In a way, though, because of this, she wished that *she* could have been the one to tell the story for a change. For the first time it actually *felt* like her story, and she knew exactly how she would tell it if she were to try. But—as Martha began her own version of things—Fay did not interrupt.

It wasn't until later, when Martha's story was long finished, that Fay remembered her daughter's question. She was gathering sheets for the daybed, where Eva would sleep, when she remembered. Martha had already gone off to bed. "So," Fay said to Eva, who was crossing from the toilet, "yes. It does get easier."

Eva had indeed forgotten the question to which Fay now referred, and only looked at her mother blankly. For some reason, this struck Fay as very funny and she laughed. For the first time in a long time she felt happy and, still laughing, she moved off to the kitchen, leaving Eva, puzzled, to take the sheets from where Fay had laid them, and go make up her bed.

ANGUS'S BULL

"I LOST ANGUS MACLEOD'S BULL," Steven said one day, charging like he was a bull himself into the kitchen. He had the same expression on his face as when he came back late after losing bad at cards. Only this time, worse. I put down the rag I had been using to mop up the sticky grape juice that Benny had spilled, and motioned to him to be quiet, though he already was.

That's what they did—he and the rest of the boys, some nights. Played blackjack or poker until someone ended up going home sorry. More often than not it was Steven who did. But really—I was lucky to have married a man with as much sense as he had. It wasn't the regular thing in our family, and so I didn't ever really mind about the money. They didn't get into any trouble, Steven and those boys. Sitting around at someone or other's kitchen table, with their hats on, and the wife of the house gone to bed upstairs. They would even be careful, because of that. Keep their voices down. Not swear too much—or loud.

I would tease him sometimes, though—worry him a little when he got back home. But mostly I just did it because it could rattle him. Nothing much did. He was the sensible type. The type to, more often than not, spend his extra money and time on things for his wife and his kid. Who didn't drink too much, or gamble too much—and you noticed it. I was lucky that way. It wasn't the regular thing.

"What do you mean you lost him?" I said.

He had that look more than ever on his face now. Like he'd forgotten where he was, or why—or what it was he'd come to say.

"He—ran," Steven said. And he made a motion with his hand to show me. The way his hand moved, though, it didn't seem to indicate a bull. More like a leaf, or a bird.

"We got a couple of the boys coming down to help," Steven said. His voice was low again, trying to sound regular, and calm. "Harley and Matthews and a couple more. Could you get them something to eat after a while?"

Then he turned around in a circle, as though he weren't sure which way was out the door.

"How long ago did you see him?" I asked.

Steven winced. "It's been a while," he said. "Could be anywhere by now."

"Well," I said. "Not anywhere." But only because it had suddenly just occurred to me as strange: even when you lost something it never did just *disappear*.

But it was a stupid thing to say, and after I said it Steven found the door quickly and hit his head with the flat of his hand as he went out, making a sound like a stuck engine. But he didn't curse. His teeth gritted together in that way, like he wanted to, but then he didn't, and the curse got pushed out instead, in a hiss, through the space between his teeth.

BENNY HAD PLAYED in the hall all that afternoon with a set of blocks that Steven had made, piling them one on top of the other until they came crashing down, making a clattering sound. When they fell like that, he would laugh out loud—and then start all over again.

But then Steven had come in with that look on his face, and Benny's own got blank and calm, like it did sometimes, and after that he didn't play with the blocks anymore, or laugh, but followed me around the kitchen with his eyes wide open. I didn't like it when he looked that way. Like he was seeing things six times over. Because then I thought about how there was an awful lot of things that he saw or would see that I didn't want him to, and that there wasn't anything I could do about it.

They tell you that: how much kids *notice* all the time, and how it sticks. They don't learn, right away, anyway, to shut things off sometimes, like we do. I wished Benny would learn quick. I hated to see him looking like that, like he was noticing everything.

ANGUS'S BULL was the best bull around, and Steven had had his eye on him for a while. "Just wait until we get that blue blood into our stock," he'd said, and showed me a picture. It was a glossy colour print, from a calendar. A blue ribbon in the corner. Angus was proud of his bull, and he charged a steep price. Steven didn't tell me how steep. It was steep enough that the boys joked sometimes about the tight rein Angus kept on that bull. Maybe feelings, they said, ran a bit deep.

But finally Steven had the money. I didn't know how. And even less what he would do about things now. Thinking of it, I began to feel so sorry for him, and for myself, that I thought I would cry. But then it seemed silly—to be crying over a bull.

I set Benny down with the blocks in the kitchen, but he didn't play. He roamed around with a few of the pots and pans that he took from the cupboards instead while I made the meal. I made a big meal: a fancy meatloaf and two kinds of potatoes. No doubt everyone was hungry.

STEVEN AND MATTHEWS, and Carol, Matthews's wife, came in about two hours after that. Harley had gone home. I'd already fed Benny and was about to take him up to bed when they came in. They didn't say much. They just banged in, and took their boots off. They all looked sad. Carol came over and gave me a squeeze on the arm and looked at Benny, and said "Aww" in this way like she knew something that he didn't know. As if it was a shame, but also sweet of him in a way, not to know it, whatever it was.

The dinner was warmed in the oven, and there were some frozen vegetables on the element, on low. I'd just put some dinner rolls on the table, and Matthews grabbed one as soon as he came in. I hadn't made them, but Steven's mother had, so they looked fresh, and homemade anyway, and gave off a nice smell.

I said, "You can help yourself to the food on the stove," and went upstairs. I made a face as I left, and nodded toward Benny, so they'd know that I wished I could stay. But really I didn't. Everyone looked too sad.

I lay upstairs with Benny and, wouldn't you know it, when I first set him down he was all of a sudden wide awake again. But then after a while he got quiet, and I sang to him some bits of the songs that I knew, like I always did. I tried not to think about what was going on downstairs. About how sad Steven had looked, or think about what it meant for us now that he'd lost Angus MacLeod's bull.

WHEN FINALLY I WENT DOWNSTAIRS, the three of them, Steven, Matthews, and Carol, were all still sitting around the table; they hadn't moved. They'd made a good dent in the food, and there was a bottle of half-finished whiskey next to Steven, and each of them had a glass.

I dragged in a mismatched chair and sat down. We didn't have a real table set yet, with the four matching chairs.

"Good meal, sweetheart," Steven said.

That's why I married him. Even when he was upset like that, he wasn't a man who'd forget to notice that the food was good, and that I'd made it.

"Thank you," I said. I hadn't eaten any of it myself, but then I felt awkward digging into the half-eaten meal when they were all finished, even though I was hungry. I thought I'd eat later, after Matthews and Carol were gone, but it turned out they stayed a long time, and more and more of that bottle got drunk, and I even helped them out a bit. Usually I didn't drink because I was still nursing Benny, even though Steven, and practically everyone else I knew, thought he was getting too old. But I knew a few things, too. Like how much stronger it could make a kid's bones. And then there were all sorts of other reasons too, so I'd kept at it. But that night I felt reckless, and thought maybe I'd quit.

"WE HAD TO SHOOT HIM," Steven said, when I'd poured my first drink and had been sitting there with them at the table for a while. "Matthews was the one to find him."

"Wasn't anything to find him," Matthews said, "he was making so much noise."

"Had his leg wedged down deep in these two stones, part of that old fence," Steven said. He looked over at me, and I wished we were alone because his face was so sad that I wanted to do something about it. "Back there—you know—"

I nodded. Maybe I would just touch his face where it was saddest. I didn't know. And then even that seemed wrong when I thought about it.

"Anyway, the leg was all splintered to bits. We had to finish it." As he spoke, Steven turned his glass in slow circles, until it began to seem as though it was spinning on its own, like a planet.

"I'm sorry," I said, even though I wished I could have said something different. But then I thought about it a little while longer, and it really did seem to be the only thing, given the circumstances, to say.

"H-yep," Steven said, taking a deep breath in on the word, and blinking around at us. "H-yep," he said again.

Carol and Matthews were drinking. No one looked around or spoke.

"This is gonna take a chunk out of our savings there, girl," Steven said to me.

He didn't call me "girl," usually, or anything cute or gruff like that. I was always just me, my own name, or else "sweetheart," which was what his mother called him, and his father called his mother, and when he said that—"girl"—I felt that maybe I was, or was to become, a different sort of person now. That we'd—both of us—have to change. Adapt. Turn out, in the long run, to be the sort of couple who had regular hardships like this. Who faced up to things, and called each other offhand names when we did so, and sometimes swore out loud, in front of the kids.

Maybe it would be easier to be like that, but, instead, up until then, we'd always just used "sweetheart" and were generally optimistic about things.

Maybe that would change, too. But though it crossed my mind that it would, I didn't really think so. I thought, instead, that after the bull was paid off or whatever would get done about it, things would go on more or less the way we wanted them to go. That we'd forget about the whole incident. That it would be an exception to the rule. Measured, and accounted for. We would, of course, have our own small allotment of troubles, just like everyone else—but no more, roughly, and probably less.

"Well, I guess there's nothing to do about it now," I said, and everyone seemed to think that was a good thing to say, too. They seemed to expect it. Like it was about time someone said it. Soberly, they nodded their heads over their drinks.

"That's right," said Carol. Then, "Honey, you look beat," she said. "I'm going to pour you another." She splashed more drink in my glass. I wouldn't have chosen on my own to drink it like that—straight up, without any soda, or a splash of hot water or something, but it didn't seem right to go about fixing that up, so I didn't protest, and just sipped it down with the rest of them. It made me feel good not to complain about it, and just do it like that.

I got drunk quickly on account of the fact that I hadn't drunk anything in so long or eaten anything since the middle of the afternoon, and then the bottle seemed to empty itself, and everyone's spirits got a little lighter.

Matthews started joking a little, about Angus. About what a stuck-up son of a bitch he was anyway, with his pin-up bull. They laughed about the glossy pictures, and made a few assertions, which were crass, and that made everyone laugh harder, and even I was laughing—though I was worried, too, about waking up Benny.

Then, suddenly, Steven got up and said he had to hit the

hay. The rest of us should stay up, he said. Finish the bottle for him.

Matthews and Carol agreed, and poured me another. So I drank it, and stayed, even though I would have liked to have gone upstairs, with Steven. Would have liked to have come back down to earth for a minute and say something like, "All that nonsense aside, what are you going to do? How are you going to tell Angus tomorrow?" But instead I had to sit there with Matthews and Carol until the bottle was gone, and by that time I was too drunk to speak at all, and so when they left, they patted me on the head and said, "You sure you're all right getting up those stairs?"

Carol giggled through her nose and her teeth. "Get him to hold yer hair back if you need to," she said. I didn't like to hear her say that to me, like we were back in high school again or something. I said, "No, no, I'll be just fine," and saw them to the door, to prove it. I did all right.

After they were gone I drank a glass of water and moved very carefully up the stairs, my hand on the wall the whole time. I realized, going that slow, that the wall was actually rough and bumpy, and not smooth at all, like I'd thought it was.

I hoped to God that this was going to be a night that Benny slept through.

When I got upstairs I fell into bed beside Steven and then crawled over and propped myself up so I was looking at him. He kind of woke up then; I hadn't tried to get in quiet. I'd just checked to see if Steven had scooped Benny up and put him in the crib, and when I saw that he had, I fell down in the bed where Benny had been. I could see, by the way that I'd fallen—quite close, with my head turned toward his—that Steven was awake. He had one eye opened and was looking at me, but in another moment—he was still that close to sleeping—he could have closed it again, and forgot.

When I saw that I had that chance, though, I started kissing him pretty hard on the mouth, and trying to get him to turn over. But he seemed heavy and not at all willing to turn. I kept kissing him anyway.

"I love you," I said. "I *fucking* love you."

I don't know why I said it like that. It wasn't what I would have said at any other time, or if I'd thought about it. But I liked the way it sounded when I said it. The swear in the middle there. Of all those nice words.

"You got drunk," Steven said. It was just a statement. There was no expression in his voice, or any reaction at all to what I'd said, or the way that I'd said it. He was probably too tired or drunk himself to care about that one way or the other.

"Do you mind?" I said. My mouth at that point was not quite—but almost—touching his ear. I could smell him. He had a musty outside smell to him. I didn't think it was a good smell, but I didn't think it was a bad smell, either. It was just a smell, and I noticed it. I kept at him. "Do you mind?" I asked again, and the words had even more shape now against his ear. He was waking up, finally. I could feel it, with how close I was to him. His muscles quickening in that way, and then he came awake for real, and said, "Hell no," very quickly, and turned over the way that I'd wanted him to turn.

IN THE MORNING I HAD a headache so I took two Aspirin. Benny was cranky and cried a lot, but I tried to pay attention to him and come up with little reasons why he was so upset.

"Juice?" I said, and remembered that I'd left the floor sticky from where he'd spilled it the day before, and would have to clean it up sometime.

But it wasn't juice, because when I offered some to him he threw it down, and cried louder than ever. This time, though, I'd given it to him in a sippy cup with a round bottom, so when he threw it down the juice just splashed around, unspilled, inside.

"What is it?" I asked Benny. I could feel my headache going away by then, as the Aspirin kicked in. With every beat of my pulse it got a little better. It was a strange thing to notice because usually you just take the Aspirin and the thing hurts and hurts until one moment it's gone.

"What is it? What is it?" I asked Benny. He didn't want to eat, or play, and he'd just had a wash, so finally I had to give up. I just held on to him, and let him cry. Let him smear his wet face and his runny nose on my shirt.

When my parents or Steven's parents were around they'd always say, "You're going to spoil that kid," but I didn't care. I didn't want to just put him down and leave him there, and have him just, like everyone else, have to "put up" with things. It seemed to me that at least for a certain time in life, when you were that young, you should be able to cry about nothing at all if you really wanted.

But it drove me crazy sometimes. I wished Benny would stop and give me some peace that morning of all mornings. I wanted to make breakfast for Steven, especially if he was going to have to go down to Angus's first thing.

But there I was, just sitting there, holding Benny, who was still sobbing away, when Steven came down, and no breakfast was made.

"Can't you do something?" Steven asked. "Can't you get him to simmer down or something?"

"Are you going down to MacLeod's?" I said, overtop of Benny's noise.

"Got to sometime," Steven said. "Be nice to eat something first." He wasn't like that usually. He wasn't snappy like that, or mean, if I just hadn't got around to something.

And I don't think that he meant to be, even then, because after he said what he said he started fumbling around with the pots and pans, and moving things in the fridge, as if all he'd meant by the remark was that he meant to rustle something up for himself before he went.

I hadn't offered to nurse Benny all that time because I'd hoped he would forget. I'd hoped I would forget, too, because I felt guilty about drinking so much the night before. But finally I gave in and Benny took to me greedily and stopped crying.

"There we go," Steven said, when things got quiet. "That's a good boy," he said. I tried not to wonder how quickly whiskey could go into the milk, or how much, and what sort of long- or short-term effects it could have on the bones or the teeth.

Then Matthews was at the door, stomping the hard clumps of dirt off his boots, outside.

"Come on in," Steven yelled, and Matthews did. He had a funny expression on his face I'd never seen before, like maybe he was going to burst into tears or else laugh out loud and couldn't decide which one was which.

"Angus won't be needing his bull anymore," he said when he came in. He just stood there in the doorway and said what he said and then kept on standing there, with that funny expression on his face.

"What?" said Steven.

"Angus won't be needing his bull," Matthews said again. "He's dead."

"What?" Steven said. He looked annoyed. "Who's dead?" he said.

"Angus," Mathews said.

"Angus?" said Steven. And then I said it too, and Matthews repeated the name again, sounding sure, and then we all just stood around for a while looking at one another. Matthews's mouth was twitching at the corners. Twitching all over the place. Like he was going to laugh, but didn't know why.

"He had a heart attack last night," he said finally, to

make his mouth stop twitching. "My mother told me. She saw the ambulance go by."

"What time?" said Steven. He had his hand up at his throat, as though he were thinking about choking.

"Around supper," Matthews said.

"Yes," Steven said. Then he repeated what Matthews had just said. He said it very slowly. Almost like a question. Or like he only understood the words one by one. That he couldn't piece them together, and so didn't understand yet what Matthews had told him.

But then I saw that just the opposite was true. That he understood too well, and was starting to see connections to things where there weren't, or shouldn't have been, any. "Oh," I said. "Don't—" and I put my hand out as if to stop him. But of course I couldn't do anything by then, so I just stood there, with my arm out, and watched his face, and saw for the first time how much he looked like Benny.

Or maybe it was just at that moment—the way he looked to me then. With his eyes wide open, and dark like that, like they were seeing things, or trying to see things, from all sides at once, and six times over.

Matthews was still standing in the door. He shrugged a little. "Guess he won't need his bull," he said again.

Steven nodded, and let his breath out in a rush. "Well," he said, "doesn't that beat all." It was not his own expression, but an old one of his father's—which, until that moment, he had used only as a sort of a joke. "Doesn't that beat all," Steven said again, in seriousness, and took one step forward. He moved deliberately. As if that were the way that a person moved and could be expected to move through life. As if he knew in what direction, precisely, he was headed, and what he'd do when he got that small bit farther forward, in the direction of the door.

Fat Man and Little Boy

SUSAN AND GINNY WERE friends from the old days. They'd worked together in the translation department of a large ball-bearing company in what used to be outside the city. Then Susan had moved to Japan and thirty years had gone by. It's funny that way. Time—without anything against which to measure itself—tends, essentially, just to disappear. A lot of things are like that; you hardly notice them, and usually for two reasons. They're either too familiar or too strange. In Japan, for example, no one ever noticed Susan's thick Maine accent in the same way—but for precisely the opposite reasons—they never noticed it in Maine. By the time Ginny finally visited, after promising to do so for so many years, Susan had taught a generation and a half of Japanese businessmen to say "watah" and "ovah theyah."

Ginny had remained in Paris all that time—far longer, now, than she had ever lived anywhere. Paris wasn't even Paris anymore, she had stayed that long; it was just a place that she lived. The city, and her life along with it, had become exactly what she had once dreaded most: *ordinary*. And even that (having nothing against which to compare itself) had lost all shape and particularity; it had crept in everywhere. That, it turned out, was what "ordinary" was.

Looking back, it was easy to see that it had, in fact, happened a long time ago. Long before Susan had gone away, even. Before anything had yet come together for either of them—or subsequently fallen apart. They had both still been young—veritable *artistes*. So sure of everything.

But if it had happened in Paris, it had certainly happened everywhere—or at least it was some comfort to assume that it had, and Ginny did. Still more comfort was to find out that this was actually the case: "You should have come ten, fifteen years ago," Susan had said when she'd greeted her in the gleaming lobby of the Osaka airport. "Things wouldn't be so—packaged up. *You* know. So—*American*."

It was a relief for Ginny to discover that the last thirty years had not had—for Susan in Japan, any more than for herself in Paris—a more noticeable, or enduring effect.

GINNY WAS, LIKE SUSAN, an American herself—from Sacramento, California. She could have joined the Daughters of Columbus if she'd wanted to. Her father had a tree at the end of the drive, the trunk of which he'd painted to look like an American flag, and even though he was now well past eighty he still touched up the paint every Fourth of July. Ginny's grandfather had almost been a real cowboy; he'd owned a ranch—only recently sold—thirty-five miles south of the city, and even with how Ginny herself had never done, as she sometimes put it, what amounted to an honest day's work all her life, this was something of which she was proud. When she visited her father, she still drove out past the Sacramento city limit to where the property—now divided into sub-plots and developments—stretched on either side of the highway. There was something that still felt vast to Ginny about that landscape. She was never sure if it was only her imagination.

By contrast, what Ginny admired in Japan was the way that everything was small. In a postcard back to Paris, she wrote that it was as if everything fit "neatly inside of everything else." Even the houses in the tidy suburbs on the outskirts of the cities, which they flew past on the bullet trains. Nothing went rambling off, unknown and extraordinary. Even the branches of the juniper trees, for instance, which when Ginny had first arrived had struck her—in contrast to the carefully tended streets—as surprisingly unkempt and wild, were, it turned out, carefully cultivated that way. Toward their own very specific, requisite immoderation. Ginny liked to see the strings still attached sometimes—evidence of their design.

Were there or were there not, she wondered, *strings*, that pulled and pushed a person in particular directions? It was her habit to feel that there were not. She was an American, after all, and did not believe in God. The great puzzle seemed, instead, to be only the manner in which, if there was no larger—outside—governing force, anything was propelled by anything at all. The future, no matter how intimately she imagined it, never seemed actually *to arrive*. It was always disappearing, instead—just out of reach.

Dissolving from what had at one time seemed (in advance of itself and independent of its approach) a *completeness*, into a procession of associative, indeterminate moments. These she was then compelled to enter into consecutively—therefore never wholly, or completely, in the way that she had once imagined.

THEY VISITED THE TEMPLES. Taking the train into Kyoto; snapping endless photographs of themselves in front of the pagodas. The evenings were spent over hot sake or wine; they had thirty years to catch up on. Through letters and emails, and the occasional telephone call, they had managed, of course, to communicate the more monumental events, which—having once occurred—or failed to occur—now constituted their lives, but now they were intent on "filling in the details." Sometimes it felt that it would take another thirty years. In that respect, not much had changed. They got on exceptionally well—just as they always had. Once, when Ginny had exclaimed at this fact in delight, Susan had coquettishly suggested she stay. As if it was true—just as it seemed. That thirty years had *not* actually passed, and they were both still able and willing to make complete and sudden changes like that in their lives.

On one of the final days of the visit, they took the train to Hiroshima to visit the museum there. It had been Ginny's idea. The one thing, she said, that she "simply had to do." She didn't say why. There was something pleasurable in not mentioning it. Not saying anything about Uncle Pauly, or Aunt Marianne—or the diagrams that Pauly had drawn into the column of the sports insert one morning when Ginny had asked him what it was he did all day while she and Marianne were out shopping, or at the cinema, or painting each other's fingernails out on the lawn. Or for that matter the particular size and shape of the cancer that was slowly killing Pauly now, while Marianne cared for him with characteristic—pretended—unconcern.

Perhaps, Ginny thought to herself—as she drifted in silence past the display cases with Susan, refraining to mention all of these things—she had expected to enter the museum as she had sometimes expected to enter the future. As usual, though, there was nothing actual or whole to enter into in the museum. It felt wrong—that there was so little to actually *do* in there, or even properly to feel. That they should emerge from it—still unspeaking for the most part, to collect their jackets at the coat check and make their way outside—so similarly to the way they'd arrived. That there was nothing to say afterward but the usual things; that Ginny herself should have gained from the experience only a sudden, nearly unbearable, fatigue.

AUNT MARIANNE WAS NOT, in fact, a blood relation, and had married Uncle Pauly when Ginny was old enough to remember. Pauly was her mother's brother, a chemist. He'd worked at the Texaco plant in Sacramento before

Ginny was born, but then had moved to New Mexico, and that was where he'd got tangled up with Marianne. "Got tangled up with" is how Ginny's mother always put it.

Still, there was nothing else to do, when Ginny's mother got sick in the summer Ginny was almost twelve, but send her down to stay with Marianne.

It was "appendicitis," they said, but Ginny knew the real reason.

Marianne drove up all the way to Sacramento to get her, and then all the way back. Ginny had never been in a car that could put its roof down. Sometimes the gas attendants or the waiters at the restaurants that they stopped at would say, "You going to try to tell me you two ain't sisters?" and Ginny would turn pink with pride.

It was a great shame—and perhaps a mistake—that the two of them were not actually blood relations. Marianne was Ginny's first truly kindred spirit, and the whole ride they hardly said a word. They would yell out together when the good songs came on the radio, and make faces at one another when they were bad. They always agreed as to which ones were which.

When they got near Los Alamos, Marianne pointed in the distance to the watchtower, which she had told Ginny about some hours before. For many years, Marianne had explained, the city had been kept under careful supervision. "It has to do with the important work that your uncle Pauly does," she'd told her. "You should be very proud." Ginny was. From a distance, the tower looked formidable, and grand. But when they approached, she saw that it was in fact now unguarded, and smaller than it had first appeared. The gates were pulled back, and the road was clear. Ahead of them, the landscape stretched—on the Los Alamos side, as on the other—repetitive and dry. There were, Ginny noted, the same moderate hills. The same distance, extending in worn-out colours: in patches of tired greens, and golds, and washed-up browns, between herself and the sky.

THE FACT WAS THAT Ginny knew all about the baby, but not about the baby dying. Her mother didn't think she knew about either. She didn't think Ginny knew about anything: that she was too young and couldn't guess, or hadn't figured anything out about life yet if her parents hadn't told her. She'd brought it up with Marianne on the first day, during the drive, even though she had wanted to pretend that it was only her and Marianne all alone in the world. She also wanted to let Marianne know that she was not exactly a child, as her mother had supposed. That she couldn't be fooled. "I know about the baby," Ginny had said, and she gave Marianne a sideways look, her hair falling over her eye. "Oh," Marianne had said, biting her lip. "Oh sweetheart, I'm sorry." And she stretched her hand out to cover Ginny's knee, her long fingernails flashing.

At first, Ginny did not understand the apology, and remained frozen, unsure, Marianne's hand on her knee. But then Marianne continued, saying: "There was nothing that anyone could do," and, "Sometimes these things happen"—and then she knew everything.

GINNY WONDERED SOMETIMES if things might have happened somewhat differently if the events of that summer had been left, instead, to Ginny's mother to explain. If it had been her mother who told her—that the baby had not been a baby at all, but only a collection of mismatched cells in the womb, which (Marianne said) could "trick you." It might have seemed, coming from her mother, different—reasonable, even. Her mother would have made it that way. She would have mentioned *God*, and then it could have been *He* that filled up the holes if there were any, and pretty soon Ginny would have again been able to enter into a—how would you say it? An understanding with the world.

There was no understanding to enter into in Marianne's car. With the top down and the baby dead, or, what was worse, never *having been*, it was clear that she could never return, now, to that other sense of things. To the faith that, up until that point, had been maintained in her by an hour and a half of church every Sunday, and a nightly emptying out of her head, which was her attempt at prayer. Instead, ever after, she would have only that sense: a long-nailed finger on her knee, and a matter-of-fact voice in her head saying that there was "nothing to be done," that "these things happened"—and always after that, too, a firm resolve that she would never, unlike her mother, be "tricked" by anything.

GINNY HAD NEVER been back to Los Alamos, but she and Marianne had managed to remain close, especially after Ginny's mother died. It was Ginny whom Marianne called, even years later, when there was anything important to say. When Pauly got sick, for example, Ginny was the first to know. One year, a forest fire had burned within five hundred yards of a nuclear storage site outside the city, and Ginny was the first person whom Marianne—a week late— told about that, too. "We drove past that spot a thousand times when you were out here," she said. "I could point it out now and you'd remember. Just out of town, right at the foot, on the Los Alamos side of the hills. You know the sad thing?" She paused and Ginny didn't say anything. "They didn't know it was going to go out," she said. "Honest to goodness, they thought it was going to burn right down the hill, right to the foundation of that building . . . No one knew what was going to happen then," she said, pausing again, and speaking hesitatingly slow, as if afraid that Ginny might not catch her meaning. "And still," she said. "No one. Said. A. Word."

Though Ginny was hazy on the details of the event and somewhat skeptical about those that she knew, she could not get rid of the image of her aunt at the other end of the line—as she had drummed out the final syllables of her story, as though they were her own long-nailed fingers drummed on her knee: "Lucky thing was," Marianne had said, "it just—*happened to rain*." Worse, still—the image of Marianne as she had apparently sat only a week before, waiting patiently in her Los Alamos living room: for the lightning flash. For the sun at once to touch the earth; for the last, dark cloud to billow up, finally, from behind the Los Alamos hills . . .

What, Ginny later demanded to know—still unable to rid herself of the image, and hoping to coax from Marianne some logical explanation, which she felt to be conspicuously missing from the account—of the unpardonable silence of the chemists and technicians? Of the government? Or even of Aunt Marianne herself? None of whom had had the clarity of purpose, or mind, to alert anyone—even poor Pauly, who was dying in the next room—that the last hour had come?

Marianne did not have any particularly satisfactory answers to offer—but nor did she defend herself, or deflect the blame. "What exactly," she had asked Ginny instead, "would you have had me say?" Then, after a long silence, amplified by the low hum of the telephone, she said: "You know, I'd rather die by flood. What about you? Or by natural fire. People shouldn't be afraid of *real things* anymore." Once more her voice was light, and untroubled—trilling slightly on her final note.

THE WAY THAT GINNY imagined it, nothing had changed in Marianne's house since the summer she was almost twelve. The photos still hung darkly. Everyone leaning a little forward in their frames. Ranchers. Ranchers' wives. Ranchers' daughters. (All Pauly's family, and therefore

Ginny's own. Marianne didn't have any family—at least not to speak of.) Generations of almost-cowboys, who, with a staunchness of character and a firmness of mind—which had become, it seemed, in ensuing generations, increasingly difficult to pass on—had crossed continents, built homesteads now long demolished, raised children now only dimly recalled . . . The land they'd cleared was still cleared land now, no doubt—a parking lot, or a shopping mall—but everything else had long since grown over or faded away. Still, though—they were men of whom a person, descended from that line, could be frankly proud; men on whom *reality*, as Marianne would have put it, fire and flood, for example, had had an effect. It seemed sad to Ginny, because of this, that on the nearly fateful afternoon her aunt had described, the one-dimensioned characters of that house had continued to regard it all—Marianne, ankles crossed, her feet touching at exactly one central point on the carpeted floor—from the ludicrousness of their over-large frames.

ALTHOUGH IN HIROSHIMA it was described as a single *instant*, there would have also, invariably, been those who had waited, like Aunt Marianne. Ginny considers this.

There would have been those, necessarily, Ginny thinks to herself—as, out from the museum, they begin to make their way across the Aioi bridge, toward the gas station, blinking, on the opposite shore—who had written the letter, tested the equipment, readied the plane . . . But, no. It was impossible to think of it. Easier, instead, to imagine the instant, the flash. Like the earth had, without warning, collided with the sun. One moment: there had been a dragonfly, alighting somewhere. And the next . . . ? Who could calculate the distance between one single moment and another? It had long seemed to Ginny that things happen not at any particular or recordable time, but at an indeterminate midpoint. Somewhere, that is, between the verifiable and measurable *tick* and the ensuing, and otherwise unremarkable, *tock* . . . in that incalculable interval of both space and time. As in the moments after a bad fall— when, for a long, extended moment that is not a moment, you are unsure if you exist at all, and it is only by great effort that you locate, at first, your elbows, your fingers, your knees, and then begin to understand again in slow successive waves that you are *alive*, returned to your body. A hand is raised, and a shout, and it is your own throat that has yelled it out—to say, before you know yourself that it is true, that you are *all right*, that no great damage has been done. And it is only in that moment of speaking, in the use of an *I*, in the channelling of a voice—your own—through a singular throat, in sending it out from its central point in the middle of your chest, that the moment comes, and you realize that you have fallen; that you have raised yourself again. And in the moment of return, the long interval (in which you felt yourself to be diffuse, hardly corporeal) disappears almost completely. You realize that, in fact, it has been only a fraction of a second, the slight effects of a shock. Hardly worth mentioning.

THE BABY HAD NOT been a baby, Marianne said, but, instead, "a cluster of cells." Years later, it was only because this description corresponded perfectly with the description of the cancer that was to cause her mother's death that Ginny realized the connection between the two things. Returning to California, after her New Mexico summer, Ginny had confided the new information to her best friend, Valerie, telling her everything she knew about the non-baby that, over the summer, her mother had not had. Valerie, though—who always thought she knew everything—had only snorted through her nose. "All babies are 'a cluster of cells,'" she'd said. "That's all anybody is." Ginny asked Marianne about this later, on the telephone, and Marianne had explained. The difference, she'd said, was that this baby's cells had been put together in a jumbled-up sort of way that made a sickness, and not a human being. It had confused, but rather comforted, Ginny to think that the line that separated what was good from what was bad was a tangible thing that could exist inside someone like her mother. It wasn't until three and a half years later, when her mother died, that Ginny realized her mistake. There was nothing, it turned out, that separated good things from bad, or that kept the bad things from happening. Still more years went by before it first occurred to her that what had happened to her mother had begun all those years ago, in the summer she had spent with Marianne and Pauly in New Mexico. Uterine cancer was the actual disease that had killed her mother, she learned, finally. Though with her own family they had always just referred to it as being "sick."

But if there wasn't a line, there were certainly still distinctions that needed to be made. That was what it meant to be a grown-up person. Still, it was appalling the extent to which a person could come to think of herself as autonomous, singular, *accountable* for certain things, but at the same time remaining always as if in between everything. Incapable, finally, of extricating herself from a sequence that led, moment to moment—always, and without recourse—to a final and inevitable conclusion. It was horrible. To think of it. Simply sitting, toes touching, and ankles crossed . . . To think of simply floating chronologically room to room, as one did in a museum. Getting closer: '43, '44. Now February, now March; just waiting, and waiting.

"FAT MAN," Susan says. They have reached the centre of the bridge, and stand, looking down at the river, which is black, and calm.

"What?" says Ginny.

"Fat man and little boy," Susan says. "Isn't that something."

They are the names of the dropped bombs, Ginny knows, but for some reason it makes her angry the way that Susan has said them. Casually, like that, and out of the blue, with the cars whizzing by over the bridge and the lights from the JOMO gas station blinking on the corner. In the end, there was only the river. And the lines of traffic on either side. The dragonfly, or not. The bicycles. The world had continued. It had gathered its relics, and proceeded on. On and on without pause. The letters, the stopped timepieces—these were only the after-effects of a thing that hadn't even happened yet. It was all, Ginny thought, just—a waiting. A waiting to end, a waiting to resume. And it continued. In the museums and the history books, which were always, inevitably (therefore) incomplete, and obscured. The ankles crossed. The carpeted floor. For lesser or greater degrees of renewal and of destruction. For the dragonfly to lift. For ourselves, finally, to realize—and with startling accuracy—the intricacies in the body of the fly, which, previously, had gone unnoticed for the wing. For example, the length of single moments. The proximity of things, object to object. Waiting; and then again, waiting, for everything to settle, and resume itself. Object to object again in a blur, moment to unchecked moment, wing to unconsidered body. Again.

IN A FEW MOMENTS, Ginny will turn and—following Susan—continue slowly to the opposite shore. For the moment, however, this is very difficult to imagine. Even her return to Paris seems remote suddenly—too much to ask. There, Ginny thinks, there will be, again, the inevitable longings, and corresponding wearinesses; the relative smallness and bigness of things. The limits—or lack thereof. She feels a sharp, caught feeling. High in her chest, as though she's drawn up—*fixed*. Pulled into sharp focus, somehow—as the T of the bridge had one time been.

Maybe she should take Susan's advice and stay. Find a small house to fit inside. Or, if that was impossible— go home instead. Repaint the flag at the end of the drive with her father for the Fourth of July. Drive out to the city limit—maybe even buy a plot of land out there. Go to the supermarket on the weekends. Bump into people she knew from high school in the aisles. Valerie, maybe. With one or two of her "clusters of cells" in tow.

But no, that was wrong, too. She could *not* just pick up and move—to Japan, this time, like Susan, or even home again, to California, if the spirit moved her. Could not begin there—wholly anew—as if an entire other life spread out before her there. That was just it. It *could not be done*, and yet—the desire persisted. In that respect, at least, she had something in common with her dimly remembered relatives—and with the world. She was caught, at that exact point of intersection between impossibility and desire. Trapped into it, just like everyone else, no matter how—or how variously—she attempted to extract herself. Without faith, and yet . . . an errant sense of direction, and of purpose, all the same. Always that—yes. The very *process* of everything as it occurred (always as if for the first time, and so without contrast) leading to the perpetual and most likely false conviction that there actually existed, at the under-layer of things, something infinitely resilient, immutable, and forgiving; that it would be possible, always, to pause . . . to defer . . . to destroy, even, if necessary; begin over again.

"FAT MAN!" Susan says again. They have once again begun in the direction of the opposite shore, Susan closest to the rail, looking down at the river, which is flat and calm. "Little Boy! It's just *sick*," she says. "To have named them something so—benign."

Ginny does not look at the river. She looks straight ahead, across the bridge instead. To the gas station at the corner, which is blinking. Then the impossible thing happens: the crosshairs, at that moment, hover and click so that of exactly that one moment she is perfectly certain. (She pauses, almost imperceptibly, her foot hovering for just a fraction of a second in the air; Susan does not alter her pace.) Prior to that, however—and of whatever happened afterward—she would never be entirely sure.

"What would you," she says to Susan, when, after a moment or two, she catches up, "have named them, then?"

ACKNOWLEDGMENTS

With many thanks to those who read these stories and offered their indispensable advice and support: Mikhail Iossel, Fiona Foster, Kate Hall, Heather Jessup, Linda Swanson-Davies, Michael Ray, and John Melillo. Extraordinary thanks, also, to my editor, Nicole Winstanley, for her belief in, and affection for, these stories. Her editorial insights, as well as those of Shaun Oakey, have greatly strengthened this work—many thanks to them both. I would also like to thank my agent, Tracy Bohan, whose support, encouragement, and friendship I am continuously grateful for. Finally, I would like to express my love and unending gratitude to John, and to my family—my mother and stepfather, Janet and Sandy; my sister and brother-in-law, Kristin and Scott, and their four beautiful children, Mairianna, Lilah, Oliver, and James.

ML   4 - 12